A SPY IN THE HOUSE OF SPAIN?

"Señor Sky-Eyes," Martínez was saying calmly, "you will please to place your weapons on the desk, very slowly."

He took a long breath. He could make a break for it, but rejected the idea. He would never reach the door.

Slowly, he reached behind him and took his belt-ax from its place. He laid it carefully before him.

"The knife, too," Martínez urged.

The blade joined the ax on the captain's desk.

"Sky-Eyes," the captain said coldly, "we think you are a French spy. Is your country pushing into New Spain?"

"Captain," Sky-Eyes pleaded, "if I were a French spy, would I carry that knife?"

The captain looked at Díaz, and both looked startled for a moment.

"Perhaps not," admitted Martínez, "but there is much you are not telling us. We will talk again in the morning. It may be that a night in a cell will help loosen your tongue."

Bantam Books by Don Coldsmith
Ask your bookseller for the books you have missed

The
Medicine
Knife

»»»»»»»»»»»

DON COLDSMITH

 BANTAM BOOKS
NEW YORK · TORONTO · LONDON · SYDNEY · AUCKLAND

All of the characters in this book are fictitious, and any resemblance to actual persons, living or dead, is purely coincidental

RL6, IL age 12 and up

*This edition contains the complete text
of the original hardcover edition.*
NOT ONE WORD HAS BEEN OMITTED.

THE MEDICINE KNIFE
A Bantam Book / published by arrangement with Doubleday

PRINTING HISTORY
Doubleday edition published April 1988
Bantam edition / October 1989

ISBN 0-553-28318-9

Published simultaneously in the United States and Canada

*Bantam Books are published by Bantam Books, a division of
Bantam Doubleday Dell Publishing Group, Inc. Its trademark,
consisting of the words "Bantam Books" and the portrayal of
a rooster, is Registered in U.S. Patent and Trademark Office
and in other countries. Marca Registrada. Bantam Books,
666 Fifth Avenue, New York, New York 10103.*

PRINTED IN THE UNITED STATES OF AMERICA

O   0 9 8 7 6 5 4 3 2

Time period: Middle seventeenth century, a few years after Return to the River

The
Medicine
Knife

»»»»»»»»»»»

I

« « »

1

» » »

It was a great buffalo hunt that year, one of the best in the memory of the People. Sky-Eyes had always enjoyed the spring hunt. True, the game was fatter during the last hunts of the fall, and the autumn sights, sounds, and smells lent a warm and comfortable charm to that season. Still, the haze of smoke from the fires as the prairie was ceremonially burned, and the quick return of the bright color to the hills made the Moon of Greening special to him.

Looks Far, the aging medicine man, had a reputation for accurate decision about the burning. No other band of the People had a medicine man whose skill approached that of Looks Far. Much depended on the timing of the fires. Too early, and the spring rains created an expanse of mud, with no new growth to the grass yet, to support the returning herds. Even grass for the horses would be scarce.

On the other hand, too late a burn would damage the grass, and grazing would be poor for an entire season, perhaps longer.

Sky-Eyes, in his first spring with the People, had questioned the medicine man.

"Why do you burn the grass?"

"It has always been so, Sky-Eyes. It is part of the medicine of the People."

"But, why? What does it do?"

"It brings back the buffalo."

1

The young man thought for a moment. Surely there was more here than met the eye of the casual observer.

"Uncle," he asked, using the traditional term of respect, "is it known how this is brought about?"

"Of course. They come where the grass is best."

"But how do they know?"

Looks Far spread his hands in a gesture of exasperation. "Where it is burned."

Sky-Eyes gave up his questioning. The conversation was going nowhere. He had learned only that the ceremonial burning of the grass was part of the "medicine" of the People. He was still at a loss to explain why. Surely, the great herds of buffalo migrated north and south, spring and fall, regardless of factors such as burned grass.

He also wondered how the medicine man decided when the proper day was at hand to set the fires. Could it be that he had some mystic vision, some spirit-message that the buffalo were so many days away? It was perhaps six or eight sleeps after the burn before the blackened hills began to take on new growth, and the prairie was resurrected from its own ashes.

No, there must be some way to tell, by the condition of the land. This would be one of the secrets handed down from one medicine man to another, through the generations. When had the first man discovered this elusive primeval truth, eons ago, that had enabled the People to establish and maintain their complex relationship with the prairie? Well, it might take several lifetimes to understand it all.

Actually, he had begun to see it in part, in a few years. It could be seen that in a burned area, the grass returned thick, lush, and uniform in texture. In small swales and isolated meadows, missed by the fire, there were more weeds and shrubby plants. Young trees invaded the prairie, in places their shade choking the life-giving growth of the nutritious crop of the grassland.

In addition, in unburned areas, tough dead stalks of last year's grasses clogged the new growth. He had watched the horses attempt to crop new green grass from among the inert husks of the previous season. It was difficult for the animals, and they soon wandered off to seek easier sustenance. He had gone to Looks Far with his discovery.

"Uncle, I would speak again of the burning time."

"Yes?"

The expression on the face of the medicine man was one of mild humor and expectation, mixed with approval. The two men had become close friends immediately, despite the differences in their ages and cultures. Perhaps it helped that Pale Star, favorite niece of the medicine man, had married the outsider. There had been many discussions between the men, Sky-Eyes attempting to reconcile his education in philosophy in the academies of France with the easy understanding of Looks Far. It had not been long before Sky-Eyes had realized that in Looks Far, he had encountered a wise teacher. More of life's meaning had been absorbed from this kindly relative of Pale Star's than at the feet of scholarly professors of academia.

Now, his metamorphosis was nearly complete. He was, to all intents and purposes, a man of the People. There was little to remind him, or anyone, that he had once been Lieutenant André Du Pres, and that he would probably be charged with treason if he ever returned to New France. Desertion, at least. He had gone the final step a few years previously, and now plucked his beard with clam-shell tweezers like the other men.

He was happy and content with his little family, a girl of eight and a boy, five. Night-Bird, with Pale Star's beauty, looked much like her mother, except for the odd gray-green of her eyes and a slight curl to her hair. The same characteristics were reflected again in the young person of Gray Fox, an active, thoughtful child.

Yes, Sky-Eyes was pleased with his status. There were only some questions that he sometimes wondered about, like that of the grass-burning ceremony. Looks Far had told him repeatedly that it is more important to feel and experience than to explain spiritual things. Still, the older man seemed pleased when Sky-Eyes grasped a new truth. Thus, he appeared pleasantly expectant when Sky-Eyes approached.

"Uncle, I think I have discovered part of the answer. About why we burn, I mean."

Looks Far merely nodded and said nothing, but he mentally noted the use of "we." Yes, his niece's husband had become one of the People, almost.

"The fire purifies the prairie," Sky-Eyes went on. "It cleans the dead growth and stops the growth of useless plants."

The medicine man smiled only a little, but his eyes twinkled as he took a long puff on his pipe before answering.

"Yes, it cleans, as rain cleans the dust in summer. But, Sky-Eyes, is any plant 'useless'?"

The young man gave a frustrated sigh. How like Looks Far to answer with another question. There was certainly no risk of one's thinking becoming stagnant with this man for a teacher.

"Maybe not, Uncle. I do not know the uses of plants as you do. But I have another question. I understand, maybe, that the buffalo look for the best food, and that is in the burned places. But how do you know *when* to burn?"

The face of Looks Far wrinkled in a broad smile, and his eyes almost disappeared in the folds of the lids.

"Ah, Sky-Eyes, that is the medicine. How to tell."

"But, there must be signs."

"Of course. And visions, too. When all the signs and all the visions are right, that is the time. Even then," his eyes twinkled again, "we miss sometimes."

2

》》》

Apparently, this year, Looks Far had not missed. His assistant circled the village three times, beating a small drum and chanting the Burning Song. Excitement had filled the air. It was one of the high points of the year, the Time of Burning.

The wind and weather must be right, to keep the fire under some control. There was a certain amount of danger, of course, which only added to the excitement. If the wind suddenly shifted, there was danger to the horse herds, to people in the open grassland, even to the village itself. One of the first lessons Sky-Eyes had been told by Pale Star when he came to the tallgrass country had to do with the threat of fire.

"It can travel faster than you, even on a fast horse. If you are threatened by fire, set a fire of your own, and then walk behind it."

It was easy to see the wisdom of this counsel, but fortunately, he had not had occasion to test it personally.

As usual, the burning went well. The flames could be watched for a long distance, winding over the hills like some gigantic serpent of fire. Many people stayed up that night, and watched the line of flames, crawling now over half the span of the horizon. It would stop somewhere, with a change of the wind, a spring shower, or a natural obstacle such as a stream.

Only a few days later, the scouts reported buffalo. They were three days to the south, an immense herd, it was said, coming straight into the burned prairie, now greening with new growth. Looks Far said nothing, only smiled in satisfaction as he returned to his lodge. Preparations were already under way for the hunt.

Spring's first hunt was in many ways the most important of the year. More so, even, than the last fall hunt, at which winter supplies were prepared and stored. The spring hunt was the first taste of fresh meat for many moons, after a winter of subsistence on dried meat and pemmican. There was a hunger, a craving for the life-giving juices fresh from the kill. Sky-Eyes remembered with amusement how he had watched the People during his first spring butchering with them. Various individuals would pause to slice a bite of warm liver and chew it eagerly. The practice had seemed so repulsive to him that he nearly gagged at the thought.

Pale Star, noting his reaction, had sliced a morsel for him. "Here. Try it. It is good medicine for springtime."

It was against his better judgment, but he would have done anything the girl asked. Manfully, he chewed the morsel. It was not, as he had feared, totally repulsive. In fact, it seemed to satisfy some deep craving for something fresh and life-sustaining.

The People were ready for the spring hunt this year, in body and spirit. It had been a bleak winter, with much snow, and food had been none too plentiful. Some families had run short, and others found ways to share their meager rations. One old woman had walked off into the storm, never to return. Sky-Eyes was horrified, but Star patiently explained to him.

Before the coming of the horse, this was a common practice. In the Moon of Hunger, when supplies ran low, it would become apparent that some must starve. To save the children, the future of the tribe, some of the older members of the tribe would walk into the prairie to die, as a patriotic gesture. Sometimes they would even sing the Death Song, usually restricted to those entering battle against hopeless odds.

> "The sky and the grass go on forever,
> But today is a good day to die!"

Now, there was little need for such patriotic self-sacrifice. With the horse, the hunt was easier, and supplies more plentiful. There were even jokes that the Moon of Hunger needed a new name.

Or, there had been such jokes, until the winter just past. Then, it was no joking matter. Warriors waded through deep snow to chop cottonwood branches and bark for their most valuable horses. All the animals lost weight, and a few died or were pulled down by wolves as they weakened and faltered.

All in all, it was a winter that the People were glad to see behind them. Never had the Moon of Awakening seemed more welcome. Geese headed north, and ice melted on the streams. Then, with the good timing of the burn, and a warm shower two days later . . . *Aiee*, the buffalo were coming, and the world was looking good once more. People readied their weapons and skinning knives and waited.

The hunt was to include most of the men in the band, and would be organized and directed by the Elk-dog Society. The Blood Society had already been acting as scouts, and would attempt to maneuver elements of the herd to a favorable location, if necessary. The Bowstrings, some of whom went so far as to prefer hunting on foot, would block a rocky hillside that offered a possible escape route for the herd.

Now it remained only for the buffalo to arrive. The Bloods were reporting frequently. There was no need to maneuver the herd, which was moving in exactly the desired direction.

"*Aiee*, old Looks Far is more skilled each season," chortled a warrior to Sky-Eyes.

"Yes," he agreed, "and his visions are good for this hunt."

The hunt would take place on the following day. Sky-Eyes strolled over to talk with his wife's father, one of the sub-chiefs.

"*Ah-koh!* White Hawk!" he called, as he approached the lodge. "It is Sky-Eyes."

The door-skin opened, and Hawk stepped out.

"*Ah-koh*, Sky-Eyes," he smiled, "are you ready for the hunt?"

"Yes," Sky-Eyes nodded. "May we ride with you?"

"You and Woodchuck? Of course. It is good."

Woodchuck, formerly Sergeant Jean Cartier, and the only other outsider in the tribe, was married to Pale Star's cousin. There had been a time of recrimination between the two Frenchmen, each accusing the other of desertion. Now their differences were settled, they had much in common, and were, in fact, closer than brothers.

A stranger was approaching the lodge of White Hawk. Both men watched him a moment. A Head Splitter, by the cut of his buckskins, thought Sky-Eyes.

"*Ah-koh*, my chief," the man began respectfully. "You are White Hawk?"

"Yes," nodded Hawk. "How are you called?"

"Lean Bear, of the Head Splitters. I was told to ask you if I may join you in the hunt tomorrow."

White Hawk, as an Elk-dog soldier and subchief, would carry much authority in the planning of the hunt.

"Of course. Another hunter will be welcome. What is your weapon?"

"The bow, my chief. I have my own horse. I was traveling, and stopped here, where I learned of the hunt."

"It is good. Be here at daybreak."

Young Lean Bear nodded and turned away. The Head Splitters, once enemies of the People, had been loyal allies since the two tribes had banded together a generation ago to turn back invaders from the north. And, in a hunt of the magnitude of this, every weapon that could be mustered would be useful.

3

» » »

Sky-Eyes sat his horse, waiting for the hunt to begin. It was a still, chilly morning, with scattered wisps of fog clinging in the low spots as the rising sun attempted to dislodge them. He shivered a little, partly from the chill of the air, partly from excitement. He shifted his grip on the lance, and found that his palms were sweating.

He glanced to his right, where Lean Bear sat toying with his bow. The young man looked over and smiled nervously. Beyond the visiting Head Splitter was White Hawk. Hawk's age was beginning to show, he noticed, in graying hair at the temples. Still, he enjoyed the excitement of the hunt, especially one as significant as this first of the spring.

On Sky-Eyes' left was the stolid figure of Woodchuck. The former sergeant preferred the bow in the hunt, riding up along the right side of a running animal to shoot. A lance hunter, by contrast, would approach from the animal's left for his killing thrust. The two had argued goodnaturedly about which was the best method. In fact, there was no single best technique. It was a choice, affected by the hunter's skill. Was he more adept with bow or with lance? Equally important, what sort of horse was available to him? One horse might prefer to pursue from the right, another from the left. Thus a different horse would be needed by a lancer than one used by a bowman. Rare would be the horse that could make the change to the other form of hunting.

The hunters were positioned along the hillside in a long

9

irregular line just below the crest of the hill, waiting. The scouts would pass the word when to advance. In general, there was a large, fairly level expanse of grassland rimmed by a wandering creek on the left and a steep rocky slope on the right. There would be men of the Bowstring Society scattered in both areas, to shoot at individual animals or to turn the herd if possible in the event of a mass movement.

One of the Blood scouts, crouching low, slipped over the ridge and trotted to White Hawk's side. The others watched eagerly while they conversed for a moment. The scout was pointing across the ridge, explaining the position of the unseen herd. He finished, and White Hawk asked a question or two, nodded, and raised a hand in signal. The scout trotted to where a friend held his horse, and swung easily to the saddle. Hawk motioned forward, and the straggling line moved ahead.

The hunt was discussed many times in the ensuing days. The events seemed accidental at the time, but who was to say? The medicine of Looks Far was known to be very powerful.

The plan was for the line of hunters to move into the herd, slowly at first, then faster as the animals started to run. They would kill as many as possible, but pursue no farther than a little way on the plain, so that the butchering sites would not be widely spread over the area.

Somehow the left end of the line came a little ahead of the rest, and the buffalo at that side of the herd began to run before the hunters were ready. It might have been a disastrous escape, but a couple of the Bowstrings along the creek happened to be in excellent position. They jumped up, arms waving, and the few buffalo which were already running shied away violently to the right, plunging into the herd. This might have brought general panic, but most of the animals were not yet excited. Instead, the tendency was to move out of the way of the few running animals. This effectively split off part of the herd from the rest. The horsemen at the left end of the line saw what was happening, and kicked their horses forward. The smaller portion of the herd, perhaps two hundred animals, began to circle, pressing in on itself. Riders took up a circling course also, beginning to drop a buffalo here and there as they tightened the circle.

It was a situation that one might dream of, with all factors, intentional and accidental, working together in perfect sequence. Those with the lance were at an advantage, since the herd was milling in a clockwise direction. Lancers could approach the left side of the running animal. Bowmen, forced to lean across the horse's neck to shoot, were having slightly more difficulty. Still, it was a wonderful hunt. The herd continued to circle, buffalo still dropping or stumbling, to lie kicking in the grass. Dust rose, choking horses and riders.

It was not until the circling herd was decimated that the survivors suddenly broke the pattern and bolted for the open prairie.

"Let them go," called White Hawk. "We have plenty!"

Tired horses turned back, riders laughing and calling congratulations to each other. The butchering parties started to straggle over the hill.

"*Aiee,* what a hunt!" Lean Bear joined the others.

His quiver was empty of arrows.

"How many?" asked Sky-Eyes.

"I do not know. My arrows will tell. And you?"

"Three, maybe four. It was better for lancers."

Everyone laughed, and they moved among the fallen buffalo, looking for the distinctive markings on individual arrows which would denote ownership of the kills. Lance kills were unmarked, of course, and ownership settled by mutual agreement.

"Sky-Eyes!" someone called. "Look at your lance tip!"

He looked and swore an obscenity that dated from another world. The razor-sharp gray flint was missing a finger's breadth from its tip. Yes, he remembered now, he had felt the strike of flint on bone when the last cow went down. In the excitement, he had forgotten to check the point, and had not made another thrust. Now, he would need a new spear head. He must talk with Stone Breaker about a replacement. Damn, this had been a good point, too. He had used it for three seasons, since he broke the last one. This was one of the minor annoyances of life with the People. It was so

easy to break or damage a favorite weapon. He longed sometimes for a good lance point of well-tempered steel. Ah, well.

He turned to look for Pale Star and Yellow Head, wife of
Woodchuck. They would need help with the heavier parts
of the butchering.

"Sky-Eyes," called Lean Bear, "I would give my kills to
you and Chief White Hawk. I will help with the butchering."

"It is good," answered Sky-Eyes. "You will eat with us
tonight?"

4

» » »

The glow of the coals shed a soft light around the circle. The scent of cooking meat still filled the night with mouth-watering suggestion, but the eating had slowed now.

There would be much work tomorrow, slicing meat into thin strips for drying, fleshing hides, and finishing the butchering. But for now, there was feasting. Darkness had effectively put an end to most of the other activities. Not until Sun Boy warmed the air could the drying of the meat begin again, so there was time to eat and relax and enjoy the day's bounty.

Sky-Eyes rose, walked to the fire, and sliced another portion of crisp-browned hump ribs from the slab at the fire. Lean Bear, the visitor, did likewise. Sky-Eyes had started to turn away when something sank into his consciousness that was not consistent. The knife in the hand of their Head Splitter guest was not the traditional flint instrument carried by most. A personal knife was a necessity for both men and women, for the numerous tasks requiring a cutting tool. Most people, unless they were especially skilled in working flint, relied on the talent of Stone Breaker.

Odd, Sky-Eyes mused, that twice today he had been made to think of this. First, when his lance point had been broken. Now, again, when he saw the knife that Lean Bear was using to assist in his eating. This was a knife of steel, its blade shining in the firelight. It was, in fact, not unlike his own.

There were only two knives of steel among the People.

13

Both had reached them by contact with the French settlements far to the northeast. One was that worn by Woodchuck on his return to the People after five years at Fort Mishighan. The other had come from there, also. It had been the only weapon possessed by Sky-Eyes and Pale Star on their cross-country journey back to her people.

And now, here was another steel knife, in casual use by a visitor from another tribe. It was not exactly like that worn by Woodchuck. This was an instrument which appeared to be of Spanish design, if his memory served. How had it come here?

"Lean Bear, this is a very special knife?" he inquired casually.

"Yes," the other replied, a little proudly. "It is a medicine knife."

He handed it over for inspection. Sky-Eyes welcomed the chance to examine it more closely. The weapon balanced well in his palm, appeared efficient, and very sharp. Yes, Spanish, beyond a doubt, and new. This was no relic dating from an early Spanish incursion into the plains. This was a recently made weapon, of the finest steel. Were there Spanish again on the prairie, new expeditions? From the information he had been able to piece together, it seemed that only occasional contact had occurred, mostly a century ago.

"*Aiee,*" he muttered, handing the knife back to its owner. "Its medicine is strong?"

He had learned that any metal object was thought to have great powers, "medicine," in addition to its primary function. Any such item took on almost a religious significance, in its contrast to the stone tools in common use. The Spanish bit, said to have been used in the mouth of the First Elk-dog, was one of the most sacred of artifacts of the People.

"Very strong medicine," Lean Bear assured him, tucking the knife back in its sheath before he sat down.

Sky-Eyes' curiosity was unsatisfied.

"How did you get this knife?"

"Trade. I gave a good buffalo horse for it."

"But where?"

"Oh. A man from another tribe had it. We camped together."

"Do you know where he got it?"

"No, but they come from the southwest. There are Hairfaces there, like your friend."

He pointed to the grizzled jowls of Woodchuck.

Sky-Eyes was thinking rapidly. He was certain that there were no French colonies in that area. The hint of Spanish influence was strong in the culture of the People. But, though there seemed to have been an early expedition or two, could there be permanent Spanish settlements within a reasonable traveling distance?

It would certainly be of benefit to the People if they had access to some steel tools and weapons. He thought again of his lance point. He had never seriously considered whether it might be possible to obtain some knives, axes, or lance points. They could not trade with the French, even if they were close enough. Both he and Woodchuck would be considered deserters. However, if there was the possibility of obtaining *Spanish* steel . . .

"Do your people trade there?" he asked.

"No, but others do, and we trade with them."

"What others?"

Lean Bear shrugged impatiently.

"Many others. Everyone trades with everyone, you know."

"Do you know the name of the place?"

"No, Sky-Eyes. Wait . . . maybe it was Sennafay, something like that."

The unfamiliar syllables seemed clumsy on his tongue.

"Anyway," he finished apologetically, "the trail that goes there runs through our country."

"A *trail* there?"

"Yes, Sky-Eyes," Pale Star interrupted. "There is a trail to the west, older than old. It goes back to long-ago times. You remember we traveled part of it the season we spent with the Red Rocks."

Yes, he remembered now. There had been so much to see and remember. He had been exploring, charting the West. They had spent a winter with the Red Rocks band of the People, camped in the shadow of the great mountains. The trail they had followed had seemed insignificant compared to everything else.

"That trail leads to the Hairface town? How far?"

"Many sleeps," Lean Bear answered. "I have never been there."

"But people from near your country go there?"

"Of course."

"Could we go there to trade?"

Pale Star saw that her husband was becoming excited at the prospect.

"We could go anywhere to trade, Sky-Eyes. But what would we trade?"

He saw her practical mind working on the matter. He remembered now that before they met, yes, even before her first marriage, Star had had extensive experience in trading. She had been kidnapped as a child, and sold to a traveling couple who had become second parents to her. They had traded from the Great Lakes to the plains and back, carrying objects of value from each area to be traded in other places. In fact, he now recalled, the first steel knife she ever saw had been the price of her bondage to Traveler. A medicine knife.

"I was thinking how great would be the good to the People," he mused, "if we could bring knives, arrow heads, maybe. We could trade furs."

"Yes," she agreed slowly, "but the season is past. Fur will not be good now."

"Suppose," offered Woodchuck, "we would take a small load of the best furs the People already have. See if it is worthwhile."

"Yes!" exclaimed Pale Star. She was becoming excited too, now. "That is good, Woodchuck."

"Wait," Sky-Eyes protested. "We must plan. We do not even know the way."

"But I can find out," put in Lean Bear. "There are those of my people who have been there. We will meet at your Sun Dance and I will take you there."

The circle of friends looked at each other in amazement at the great step they were considering. Finally, Woodchuck broke the silence with a chuckle.

"It is good!" he exclaimed.

5

» » »

There was much more talk that night, much laughter and excitement. White Hawk watched them and listened and chuckled.

"I would go with you if I were younger," he encouraged.

Plans were outlined for the upcoming venture. Lean Bear would return to his people and attempt to learn all he could about the trail to the west. The others would assemble a pack of furs from their own band of the People, and begin to select horses for the journey.

They would meet at the Sun Dance, in the Moon of Thunder, as Lean Bear had suggested. The Head Splitters had no Sun Dance of their own, but often attended that of the People. After the Sun Dance and the Big Council, they would travel with the Red Rocks, branching off on the old Westward Trail at the appropriate place. This plan would provide three moons to assemble furs and other items for trade, and give Lean Bear the opportunity to learn more about the trail itself.

A question that required more debate was that of who should go on the expedition. It was quickly agreed that Pale Star would be valuable because of her trading experience. This in turn implied that her husband, Sky-Eyes, would accompany her. But what about their children? This might be a dangerous mission, and the children's safety should not be risked. They could stay with relatives.

Yellow Head, wife of Woodchuck, would be a logical

guardian for the children of both families while the men were gone. Woodchuck, however, was reluctant.

"What if we do not return? Yellow Head would be left with two families and no husband."

"You just want to be with me!" Yellow Head accused.

Everyone laughed. The closeness of this couple was a source of much amusement among the band, and not a little envy.

"Maybe so," admitted Woodchuck self-consciously, "but I still think we should not risk our families' safety."

Finally, a compromise plan emerged. Both families would travel with the Red Rocks after the Sun Dance. Then Sky-Eyes and Pale Star would form the trading party, while Woodchuck and Yellow Head stayed with the children among the Red Rocks to await their return. Woodchuck viewed this with mixed feelings. He felt torn between responsibility to his family and the call of adventure.

"You should have another man or two," he suggested.

"Yes," Sky-Eyes agreed. "Who should go?"

"Maybe one from our band and one from the Red Rocks," suggested Star. "They should be allowed to share."

Exactly what they would share was, of course, a great question. There was much risk, of property loss as well as life and limb. They agreed to approach the subject quietly with selected members of the band. Not until the trading party was selected would they start to ask for furs to trade. The number of people to go west would be limited to six, including one more from the Head Splitters, to be chosen by Lean Bear.

At this point Star began to be concerned about the size of the party, though she had originally suggested an extra person or two.

"When I was with Traveler, there were just the three of us, and then just two after Plum Leaf's death."

"But this is unknown country," her husband insisted.

"Traveler traded in unknown country."

"Yes, and Traveler is dead," he reminded gently.

"It was for other reasons, though," she answered stiffly. "But, no matter. It is probably safer to take more people. And, we will carry more trading goods than Traveler did."

One factor that they had not counted on was the enthusiasm of others for the project. Everyone seemed to have something to send. Finally, it was necessary to make decisions as to what might be taken. Star and Sky-Eyes were called on to accept or reject, she because of her trading experience, and Sky-Eyes for his knowledge of what the Spanish might desire in trade.

He felt quite inadequate in this regard. It had been nearly ten years since their last contact with their own French settlement, and who knows what a Spaniard will want? He tried to limit the selections to furs, which he knew had almost universal appeal, and a few carefully chosen and tanned buffalo robes. These items would serve as examples of available trading stock for the future.

He rejected a pair of beautiful beaver pelts because they had been cut in the wrong places for skinning.

"I am sorry, Uncle. They must be cut so, and then stretched round on a hoop of willow."

"But why, Sky-Eyes? A beaver is not round!"

"I know. But that is the way they are stretched among the people across the Big Water."

"There are beaver there, too?"

"Yes, but very few. This is why they will buy ours."

Of that, he wished he felt more certain. But surely the market for furs was as strong as ever. The search for gold which had been an early impetus in the exploration of the New World had faded now. Spain had taken much gold, but France and England were thrusting into the continent with furs as their main object.

Strange, he mused. He had not even thought about the intricacies of European politics for years, now. It was part of another world, one he had left behind.

"Mother," Star was smiling as she spoke to an old woman, "the quillwork on these moccasins is the finest, but we do not know whether the Hairfaces need moccasins. I will ask, and take them next year if they wish to trade for them."

She did select a beautifully·tanned robe of wolfskin from the same woman. It was difficult to know what would be wanted.

Choice skins of otter, beaver, wolf, spotted cat, and, yes,

even of smell-cat were assembled. They tied similar skins in bundles, to be packed on horses or placed on the platforms of the pole-drags. "Travois," Woodchuck called the pole-drag, borrowing a word from his own tongue. There was much discussion on this point.

"A horse can drag more than he can carry," observed White Hawk.

"Yes," Lean Bear agreed, "but we will cross mountains. I do not know if we can drag where the trail leads."

To the People, accustomed to traveling on the open prairie, the pole-drag seemed thoroughly practical. Wide at the rear end, the device could be maneuvered along most trails of the plains, or through areas without trails in the rolling grassland. It was hard for them to visualize a trail through narrow, rocky clefts, which it would be impossible to go around.

"We will ask the Red Rocks," Lean Bear suggested diplomatically.

But meanwhile, he, Woodchuck, and Sky-Eyes started training a few horses to wear pack saddles and carry loads on their backs.

6

» » »

The atmosphere at the Sun Dance was always thrilling to
Sky-Eyes. It was a combination of the best of times in his
youth back in France, a mixture of the excitement of a country fair and the emotion of a religious holiday.

Except, he had to observe, the People seemed to enjoy
their religion more. In retrospect, his own religion had been
serious, even somber. Anything which seemed enjoyable or
amusing had been frowned upon as sacreligious. It was not
so here. The Sun Dance was a thing of joy, of reunion, a
celebration of the return of the grass and the buffalo. The
five days of the dance brought forth expressions of thanks-
giving, supplication, restoration of health, of patriotism all
rolled into one.

Aside from the ceremonial dances, there were the social
contacts with other bands, family visits, games, contests,
and romances. At any given time, it was possible to look out
across the prairie and see groups of young horsemen demonstrating their ability, wheeling, charging, yelling, racing in
the fullness of youth.

Also, behind the scenes were the plans for the coming
year. Where would the next Sun Dance be held? What
would be the site for each band's winter camp? Who would
camp with which relatives for a season?

Into this exciting and special holiday atmosphere came
those planning the trading expedition. Lean Bear arrived a
day late, after the Dance had begun. This was of no matter,

as the Head Splitters attended by choice, and largely as observers rather than participants. It was not unheard of for one of their tribe to participate in the dance, or even to make sacrifices, but it was not common, either.

In this case, Lean Bear and the others were too busy to participate actively. They were collecting and packing furs and skins for the expedition. Pale Star did sacrifice an exceptionally fine otter skin in behalf of them all, and they asked the visions and prayers of Looks Far for their undertaking.

There was much excitement in the tribe over the coming journey. They turned down several requests by young men who offered their services to go along.

Lean Bear also brought news of his inquiries about the trail.

"It is very old, as we said," he reported. "Our people call it the Westward Trail. It goes to the mountains."

"The mountains?" Sky-Eyes interjected. "Do we want to go there?"

"Of that, I am not sure. This village, Sennafay, lies to the south. We go to the mountains, then turn south, through a cleft or slash, on south to the village."

"How do we find the way?"

"Ah," he smiled, "that is the best! I have a cousin who has been there. He will go with us."

"Where is he?"

"With our people. He is gathering some furs, and he will join us when we stop there."

"And he knows the way?" Pale Star was insistent.

"Yes, of course. He even knows another way."

"Another?"

"Yes. We did not talk much of that. It is shorter, but more dangerous."

"The people there are dangerous?"

"No, I think not. Maybe. He said there is no water."

"Well, we will see. He can tell us more," Sky-Eyes observed.

"Yes, that is better," agreed Lean Bear, relieved. "I cannot answer all the questions."

Even so, he did remember other things from time to time.

"My cousin says the people at Sennafay are mud-lodge people."

"I thought they are Hairfaces," questioned Sky-Eyes, alarmed at this news.

"Yes, yes, of course, Sky-Eyes. It is a Hairface town, but others live nearby."

"The tribes in that country are mud-lodge people," Pale Star attempted to clarify. "Their lodges are made of mud and poles, not of skins like ours."

The concept was very difficult for the Frenchmen to accept, until they remembered that the People's word for their own skin dwellings was also used for any dwelling of any sort. A heron's nest or a mouse's burrow, or a fox's den, all were a lodge, a home. Even the setting sun was described in such terms. "Sun Boy goes to his lodge on the other side of the earth." Well, it would eventually be understandable.

"I know!" exclaimed Pale Star. "Sky-Eyes, Woodchuck, you know the lodges at Fort Mishi-ghan?"

She sketched a square with a finger.

Log cabins, and a log palisade. Was this what they were trying to describe?

"Yes," her husband nodded tentatively.

"The shape is the same, but they are made of mud, not logs."

"Oh. I see."

At least, he thought, I think I do. He was thinking of the sunbaked bricks used for building in other parts of the world. This raised a new question. Had the Spanish brought this method here, or had the natives, the "mud-lodge people," known it already? It was an unanswered question for the present.

It was not until after the ceremonial Sun Dance, when most of the official duties of the medicine man were over, that they approached Looks Far for his help. He readily agreed to try for a vision.

Now they must wait, and not contact him again about the undertaking. The vision must come in its own time. Sky-Eyes became impatient. The Sun Dance was ended, the Big Council was over, and in a day or two the tribe would disperse. Looks Far would go with the Elk-dog band, while they would be heading west with the Red Rocks. He voiced his concern.

"Do not worry," assured Pale Star. "Looks Far knows that. He will do his best."

Even so, it was the morning of their departure before Looks Far approached them with a smile. Some of the lodges were already coming down in preparation for departure.

"*Ah-koh*," the medicine man greeted. "I have had your vision."

"Tell us, Uncle."

"I am made to feel that it is good. There will be hard times, but the plan is good."

"There is danger?" Pale Star inquired.

"Maybe. There is always danger. But you are strong. You have all faced danger before."

Somehow, there was an eerie quality in the predictions of Looks Far's visions. Sky-Eyes always had the feeling that the old man could actually see through the window into the future, and watch events that were to come. His background and education told him that this could not be. Still, it was quite comforting to hear of favorable visions regarding the upcoming expedition.

"Thank you, Uncle," he said quietly.

7

» » »

The two pack horses moved well after the first day of travel. It was necessary to adjust the padding of the saddle on one of the animals on the third day to prevent chafing. After that, however, they settled into a routine of travel. It was pleasant to be with the Red Rocks again. They had many friends in this band.

Woodchuck had a few memories to deal with. Their last season with this band had seen him with a new bride. Pink Cloud had been killed, in fact, while they were hunting with the Red Rocks. But that was nine summers ago. He had been with Yellow Head for four seasons now, and she was more than a mother to his son by Cloud. Red Feather, the youngster was called, after his grandfather, chief of the Eastern band. Most people, however, still called him Ground Squirrel, the small Woodchuck, because of his resemblance to his father.

They hunted occasionally when the opportunity offered, but it was not a serious thing. There was no time when they were traveling to stop and dry meat, or to dress skins. It was a matter of a kill or two for fresh meat to be shared by the entire band at the night's camp, without attempt to save and preserve any.

"Star," her husband asked as they rode one morning, "when do we reach the Westward Trail?"

"We are traveling on it now," she laughed. "There are

several branches and forks. Soon we will come to the river, the Ahr-ken-zes, and then we follow it."

The Red Rocks, she explained, had elected to move somewhat farther south this season, to accommodate the trading venture. They did reach the river, and the trail became plainer now, sometimes following the river's bank, sometimes taking a shortcut across a long loop of the stream. It could be seen for long distances, marked by a dark green fringe of trees wandering through the lighter green of the prairie grasses.

There were also places where those following the trail had apparently disagreed with those who had gone before. A side trail would wander off, only to return to the main route in the space of a few bow shots, or even a hundred paces. Sky-Eyes mentioned this to his wife.

"Yes. Maybe it was muddy sometimes on the lower trail."

She pointed ahead to a low spot, where dozens of yellow butterflies swarmed to suck the life-giving moisture from the earth.

"Travelers took the hillside path. Then, the trail dried, and they began to use the shorter way."

He had always thought of a trail as a line stretching between two points, by the most direct route. Now, he was beginning to see that it was more like a loosely tangled bundle of strings, each traveler taking the path that seemed most practical to him on that particular day. In retrospect, the thing seemed obvious, that the trail might even split into several paths in a rough area, to rejoin beyond.

This made him think of something Lean Bear had said, that there was another way to the village of Sennafay. He asked Star about it.

"I do not know, Sky-Eyes. I think the trail branches farther west."

"For more than a little way, like this?"

He pointed to a division that ran separately, one route along the hills and another in the bottoms, for a half-day's travel. They were on the hillside, and could see both branches for a long way.

"No, more than this. Many sleeps, I think. Do not be impatient, Sky-Eyes. We will see."

He had also noticed another thing. The country was changing. He had observed this on their previous trip west ten years before, but more so this time. The vegetation was different. It was still prairie, with grass in the great expanse of earth as far as eye could see in all directions. The streams were still marked by wandering lines of cottonwood and willow, but there were different grasses here.

Before he came to the prairie, he had thought that grass was simply grass. It took no longer than the first autumn with the People to realize the error of that idea. There were grasses of all different heights. The tallest, called real-grass by the People, sometimes raised its seedheads well above a man's height. Nearly as tall was that called plume-grass or feather-grass, with fluffy yellow heads nodding in the breeze. Others were mixed in abundance, varying in heights and in types of seedheads. He had once counted seven or eight completely different grasses in an area only a few paces across.

In the region where they were now traveling, the big grasses of the Tallgrass Hills were scarce. The predominant type was a short blue-green curly-leaved grass which their companions referred to as buffalo-grass. Scarcely a hand's breadth in height, it formed a thick tangled mat. He now recalled that the People referred to the western portion of their range as the "shortgrass plains."

In some areas, even the short grass refused to grow. Rocky or sandy stretches showed whitish streaks in the gullies and dry stream beds. At one pool, the leaders of the caravan did not even pause to allow anyone to water horses.

"It is bad water," explained Star. "Makes horses and people sick. Tastes bitter."

Sky-Eyes was willing to take her word for it. When Pale Star told him something about the Prairie, he had found that he could count on it. Unless, of course, she was teasing him, and he could usually tell that.

Lean Bear rode up beside them.

"Tomorrow we will find my people," he announced. "They will be camped on the river, they said."

"Will your cousin and the pack horse be ready?" Star asked. "I do not know if Sky-Eyes can wait."

They all laughed, even Sky-Eyes. His eagerness to proceed with this venture had become a joke among the band.

"I think so," assured Lean Bear. "Turkey Foot will know we are ready to go on."

"Do we leave the Red Rocks here, Lean Bear?"

"No. They will go on west with us until nearly at the mountains."

"Then they turn north, and we turn south?"

"Yes. Something like that. Not exactly the same place."

"Where is the other trail you spoke of?"

"Oh yes. That is just west of here. But we cannot use it. There is no water at this time of year."

A rider was approaching from in front of the column. He appeared to be one of the "wolves," or advance scouts. A band on the move had men as outriders on all sides, observing for danger. Wolves, they were called, because a band of buffalo on the move was always circled by a few big gray wolves. This similarity to the circling scouts, though for a far different purpose, was noted in the expression. The scout now drew up before the Red Rocks chiefs and pointed ahead.

"The camp is there," he announced. "We will be there before dark."

8

» » »

The two days that the People camped near the Head Splitters was a time of great interest to Sky-Eyes. He had not had the opportunity to visit one of the villages of the other tribe before. A generation ago, he had been told, the two were enemies. They had banded together to fight the common threat of an invader from the north. One of the major figures in the story, he had been told, was Looks Far himself. He and a young medicine man from the Head Splitters had worked together, using their different skills for the same purpose. As the story was now told, there was much of magic and the supernatural. The entire tribe of invaders had been defeated without a battle, as the combined medicines caused a stampede of buffalo to destroy them.

"Come," Star told him after they were settled, "we will pay our respects."

She took him by the hand and led him toward the Head Splitter camp. Sky-Eyes was a little confused. He knew that there was an intricate protocol in visiting a village other than one's own. It was important to pay respects to the chief. But surely, in this situation, their own chief, Yellow Horse of the Red Rocks, would be the one to make the diplomatic contact for the band.

"We go to see the chief?" he asked.

"No, no," Star laughed. "Bear and Yellow Horse will do that. This is a friendship visit, to the medicine man."

"The medicine man?"

"Yes. I promised Looks Far that we would visit his friend Wolf's Head. They stopped the Blue Paints, you know."

"*That* medicine man? He is here?"

"Yes, Sky-Eyes. I have asked Lean Bear. This medicine man is old, but his head is still good."

What an opportunity, thought Sky-Eyes, to know not only one, but both of the miracle workers in the great event commemorated in song and dance.

"Do you know him?" he asked.

"No, unless I saw him when I was very small, before I was stolen. I think not."

He saw that Star, too, was excited over this opportunity.

"Do you speak their tongue? How will you talk to him?"

"No, I have never learned much of their language. But Wolf's Head speaks our tongue, it is said. We could use sign-talk, of course."

They stopped before a large lodge with many decorative designs. A shield hung on its pole beside the doorway, with a wolf's head as a decorative design. Star tapped on the lodge skin.

"*Ah-koh,* my chief," she called ceremonially, in her own tongue. "We bring greetings from your friend Looks Far."

There was the sound of someone moving in the lodge, and a woman looked out the door. She withdrew, and there was a rapid exchange of words in a foreign tongue. Then a man's voice called out.

"Welcome! Wait, I will come out."

The door-flap lifted, and an elderly man stooped to come out.

"*Ah-koh,*" he smiled. "Let us walk to the shade near the river. It is hot in the lodges. Now, tell me, daughter, how are you called?"

"I am Pale Star, Uncle. This is my husband, Sky-Eyes."

"Ah yes. Looks Far told me of you. You are the one who was stolen. They thought you dead."

"You have seen Looks Far while I was away, then?"

"Yes, but many seasons ago, before your return. All thought you dead except Looks Far. He knew. He told me, told me you were special. He is your kinsman, is he not?"

"Yes. He told me much of you when I was small."

"You asked many questions, he said. 'How do buffalo know where the grass has been burned—do they have visions?' "

The old man chuckled. They had reached a shaded area near the water, and Wolf's Head sat on a fallen tree.

"Now, let me look at you more carefully. *Aiee*, you are beautiful! I wish I had met you when my eyesight was better."

He turned to Sky-Eyes.

"And this is your husband?"

Sky-Eyes was embarrassed and a little confused. How was it, that even with failing vision, it seemed that this man could look right through to his soul? It was like his first meeting with Looks Far. Sky-Eyes found himself fervently wishing the approval of the medicine man.

"Does Looks Far approve?" he asked Star, who was trying to conceal her amusement.

"Yes, Uncle. They are good friends."

"It is good," announced Wolf's Head, as if it were a verdict. He turned back to Sky-Eyes.

"Where is your tribe?"

"Across the Big Water, Uncle."

"Yes, I thought so. Your eyes, they give you no trouble?"

He had been through this before. The first of the People he met had considered him blind.

"No trouble," he smiled. "I can see quite well. Many of my people have blue eyes."

"Yes, I have heard. But yours must be a different tribe than the ones to the south and west of us, the Hairfaces?"

"Yes, Uncle, there are several tribes. We go to trade with these."

"So I have heard. Do you know them?"

"We have not been there yet. I know their tongue."

"Good." He turned to Pale Star. "Did you know they seldom use our sign-talk?"

"No, Uncle. It is good that my husband speaks their tongue, then."

Sky-Eyes had another thought.

"Looks Far's vision was good for our venture," he offered. The wrinkled face broke into a broad smile of approval.

"Good. He saw any danger?"

"Some, but success, too."

Wolf's Head nodded.

"I will try for a vision, too."

"That is very kind, Uncle."

"It is nothing. You are family, almost. Has Looks Far told you how we met? There were these invaders, the Blue Paints, very cruel and without mercy. They were moving into our country, were already in your Sacred Hills. Did they not nearly destroy your Northern band? Yes, I thought so. Your people and mine were enemies then, you know, and . . ."

The shadows grew longer and twilight fell before they made their way back to the camp of the Red Rocks. They said little to each other. It was plain that both had felt very deeply the influence of this remarkable man.

André Du Pres, now Sky-Eyes of the People, even with all his formal education, felt as he always had in the presence of Looks Far. Here was another teacher and philosopher from whom he could learn, if he had the time to do so.

"I am happy that we talked with him," he said quietly to his wife.

She nodded in the darkness.

"Yes. He is much like Looks Far. I can see how their medicine could work together."

9

» » »

Their short stay with the Head Splitters called one thing firmly to the attention of Sky-Eyes. This was a different tribe, with different customs, but their culture was much like that of the People. They hunted the buffalo in the same way, and their lodges, garments, and weapons were similar. A few differences were noted. The shape of the door-openings in the lodges, the pattern of moccasins, the cut of a garment might distinguish the two, but the basic culture was the same. Their livelihood depended on the buffalo, and thus on the horse.

It was no wonder, the reverence with which the People regarded Heads Off, the hero of a century ago, who had brought the First Horse. In a way, he had saved the tribe from the annual threat of starvation. Sky-Eyes wondered if all the hunting tribes had such a heroic figure as part of their legendry, from the time they acquired the horse. He asked Lean Bear about it.

"Bear, how did your people find the horse?"

Lean Bear shrugged.

"We have had them since before I was born."

"Yes, I know. But where did they come from? Our First Horse was brought by Heads Off."

"Oh yes. Our scouts saw some Hairfaces riding horses. They followed and saw that it was good, the dog as big as an elk, wearing a turtle on each foot. Finally, they were able to steal a few, and these had young. That was about the same time as your tribe and Heads Off."

This confirmed his suspicions. Every tribe must have its own legends of the horse, its origin, and the circumstances involved. He remembered with amusement the surprise with which he had discovered the Spanish influence on the plains. At that time, he had been documenting information to be used in the conquering and colonization of the New World. How unimportant that seemed now.

There was one major cultural clash that occurred while the Red Rocks were camped with the Head Splitters. It was just at daylight, and they were aroused by the barking of dogs, shouts and yells, and general excitement. Sky-Eyes and Woodchuck seized weapons and ran toward the other camp. Was this an attack of some sort?

"What is it?" they began to ask the people they encountered as they ran.

At first they received only blank looks, and quickly realized that most of the Head Splitters did not know their tongue. They paused to inquire in sign-talk.

"They are chasing a bear!" grinned an excited old woman. "It walked into camp!"

Both men were immediately uncomfortable. The People did not kill bears except in emergencies, and even then did not eat bear meat. To the People, a bear walks erect like a man, and so must be nearly human. To eat bear meat was practically cannibalism. It was a tribal taboo, its origin lost in antiquity.

They paused and listened to the sound of the chase in the trees along the river. There was a pause and an increase in the frantic barking of the dogs, then a sudden yelp of pain. The harried animal had turned on its tormentors, and at least one dog had learned the danger of the slashing claws.

Pale Star ran up behind them.

"A bear," her husband informed her. "What should we do?"

"Nothing. It is theirs to do. If they kill it, they will have a feast tonight."

It had been a hard concept for Sky-Eyes to grasp. In his experience in his own country, when two cultures came in contact, each tried to force its beliefs on the other. There was none of that here.

He recalled the first time he had seen Pale Star, long ago in Mishi-ghan. She was attempting to exchange stories with another storyteller, who happened to be a Jesuit priest. She was indignant that while she and the others had listened admiringly to his story of creation, he was unwilling to hear theirs. It had been amusing, but significant to young Lieutenant Du Pres. These people respected the beliefs of others, even when in conflict with their own.

Judging from the sound, the bear was moving again. There was a great splashing as the animal made its break to cross the river. Dogs and human pursuers were placed at a disadvantage at once. There was no way in which they could traverse the knee-deep river as fast as the bear, either swimming or running.

They caught a glimpse of the shaggy black creature as it scrambled up the other bank and disappeared in the fringe of willows. It would keep moving, they knew, until safely away from the camp.

They turned to make their way back to their own camp. It was somewhat behind them now, as they had followed the chase downstream for some distance. A thicket of willows grew in a low spot just to their right, and now a sound from that cover made their neck-hairs stiffen. It was a low, snarling growl.

Sky-Eyes had not thought of this possibility, that there might be another bear. All three had stopped short almost in midstride, and now turned cautiously to look in the direction of the sound. The willows stirred, and the dark shaggy creature rose to full height, snarling again at the intruders.

It appeared to be a yearling male, probably the twin of the other animal. It was somewhat unusual for it to stand this way, to threaten on its hind legs. A real-bear might, but as a rule the black bear, if it meant to attack, would simply charge on all fours. Sky-Eyes gripped the lance he had grabbed in the excitement of danger, and readied himself for defense.

"Wait," whispered Star. "Let Woodchuck talk to him."

The sweating Woodchuck stepped forward, bow at the ready.

"I will try."

Woodchuck seemed to have an ability to communicate that was beyond that of most.

"*Ah-koh,* my brother," he began quietly. "We do not wish to harm you, but will if we must."

A low growl of challenge was the only answer.

"I will turn away, and you can do the same," Woodchuck offered.

The bear lowered its head, still threatening, and snarled again.

"Go now, join your brother," Woodchuck pleaded.

The animal seemed unsure, but sank slowly to all fours. For a moment it seemed ready to charge, but then turned with a final snarl and disappeared into the brush along the stream. A moment later, they saw the dark form, half wading, half swimming, crossing the river.

"*Aiee,* Woodchuck, you talk well!" exclaimed Star.

It was an ability that the big man seemed to have.

"It is nothing," he murmured self-consciously.

"Tell me, my friend, when did you first do this?" inquired Sky-Eyes.

"I do not know how it began," Woodchuck answered. "I talked to a real-snake once, and it helped me later."

There might have been a time when André Du Pres would have scoffed at such ideas. Sky-Eyes, however, now nodded in agreement.

"It is a gift," he acknowledged.

"Yes, use it wisely," said a voice behind them.

They turned to see Wolf's Head standing near. How had he approached so quietly? Sky-Eyes wondered.

"You do not need my visions now," the medicine man continued. "You have good medicine for your journey."

"But Uncle," protested Woodchuck, "I am not even going."

"No matter," Wolf's Head dismissed the objection with a wave of his hand. "They will carry your medicine with them."

10

» » »

Turkey Foot, cousin of Lean Bear, proved an ideal choice for a companion on the journey. He was cheerful, intelligent, and pleasant to be with. He had understood immediately the problems and goals faced by the expedition. His pack horse seemed steady and well trained, and the stout buckskin that he rode equally so.

"Is he a buffalo horse?" asked Sky-Eyes.

"Yes, he hunts well. I use the lance for buffalo. But for this, I chose him because he rides comfortably."

A sensible conclusion, thought Sky-Eyes. He also wished to talk of the route to the Spanish settlement.

"Tell me, how is this trail?"

"It is good. I have been there only once, Uncle, and then only as far as the Hairface village, but I can take you there."

Sky-Eyes tried to ignore the use of the term "Uncle," which referred to any older male of the People. He realized it had been used only as a term of respect, but it implied age. It was a new feeling for Sky-Eyes. He changed the subject.

"Tell me of this other trail, the one Lean Bear spoke of."

"Oh, the Desert Trail? It branches off the main trail just west of here. I will show you. But, we cannot use it."

"Because there is no water, Bear said."

"Yes. In some seasons there is water, but not in the Red Moon. Now the rivers run upside down."

The Red Moon. August. Driest of the year on the plains.

37

But what about the strange expression just used by Turkey Foot?

"Upside down?"

"Yes, Uncle. There is water, sometimes. By digging in the sand of the dry stream you can find enough sometimes, maybe. But it is not sure."

But good to keep in mind, to remember, Sky-Eyes thought. It might be useful someday.

In two sleeps the Red Rocks started on, with the trading party, now complete, accompanying the column. Sky-Eyes, with the old skills of the military still working unconsciously, evaluated the little caravan as they rode. The two more who had joined them, Crow of the Elk-dog band and Beaver Tooth of the Red Rocks, seemed well chosen. Already the six were working satisfactorily together, loading and unloading the three pack horses for the night stops.

"There is the Desert Trail," pointed Turkey Foot on the third day. "See, you would cross the river there, just below the little island, and head southwest."

Sky-Eyes could see how it would be possible to cross the river on the sandy shoal, but beyond that, the trail seemed nonexistent. The wide expanse of sand, studded here and there with soapweed, shimmered like water in the afternoon sun. He saw no track at all. A traveler would have difficulty even starting in the right direction.

"But where is the trail?" Sky-Eyes asked, a little bewildered.

Turkey Foot laughed. "I said it is dangerous."

"But it does lead to the same place?"

"Oh yes, I have seen it at the other end. But we follow this branch, to the west."

The river became more shallow as they moved to the west, but its bed was broad and sandy. Sky-Eyes was continually fascinated by the changing country. While the broad expanses of the rolling plain were treeless, gigantic cottonwoods grew along the streams. Sometimes they were alone, a single sentinel visible for half a day's journey. Others were seen in groups of five or six, forming a grove of their own, with filtered shade to rest the travelers for a little while.

Sky-Eyes attempted to estimate the size of one lone giant,

using almost forgotten skills from his other life. It would have taken at least four men linking hands to circle the tree at its base. The height, using the military method of estimation, would be easily twelve times his own height.

There finally came a day when the Red Rocks would turn north. The children of Sky-Eyes and Pale Star were eager to join the lodge of Woodchuck and Yellow Head for a season. They were near the same age, and had grown up together, with young Ground Squirrel.

Sky-Eyes and Woodchuck walked a little apart on the night of the last camp before parting.

"You will be careful, my friend?" Woodchuck asked, concerned.

"Of course. We should have nothing to fear from the Spanish. We are not at war with them, as we are with the English."

"By 'we' you mean the French, I suppose."

"Well, yes, I did," offered Sky-Eyes, a trifle confused.

"But, you are not French, but a man of the People, a trader."

"Yes, that is true, Woodchuck. It will be best. I guess a trader of the People could speak Spanish."

"I suppose so. There must be many natives who speak Spanish at this place Sennafay."

Suddenly a thought occurred to him, and he chuckled in glee.

"Woodchuck! Listen, my friend, that name, 'Sennafay.' I thought it was a native word. It must be Spanish! They are saying 'Santa Fe.'"

They returned to the camp, and inquired of Turkey Foot.

"Tell us, the name of this Hairface town, it is Santa Fe?"

Turkey Foot looked bewildered.

"Of course. Did Bear not tell you? It is the tongue of the Hairfaces, 'Sennafay.'"

Somehow, this evidence of Spanish culture lent more credibility to the venture. Spaniards were a known quantity, people of a neighboring country back home, while tribes in the area were an unknown.

"Be careful anyway, Sky-Eyes," admonished Woodchuck.

"We know how a Spaniard might treat a French officer, but not how he will treat a native trader."

Sky-Eyes considered a moment, then smiled.

"Well, if one is not successful, I can be the other."

"Yes, maybe. But consider, my friend, you do not know how a French officer will be treated by the natives, either."

"That is true, Sky-Eyes," his wife added. "We must move very cautiously until we see how the wind blows."

The next day the Red Rocks moved north and the trading party moved south. Six riders and three pack animals, moving into the unknown. On the far distant horizon to the west, vague shapes of mountains could be seen, lying blue against the lighter blue of the sky.

11

» » »

The six travelers became better acquainted in the ensuing days. They moved through unfamiliar country, where only Turkey Foot had been before. Scrubby junipers clung to the red-brown slopes or in unlikely crevices of the rocks. Grass was sparse. In fact, there was little vegetation beyond short, brushy growth, thinly scattered.

There were small creatures of unfamiliar kinds that scampered through rocky crevices and perched on boulders to call to each other. Birds unlike any in their own experience fluttered fearlessly near the travelers, even lighting on their packs when they stopped to rest.

"*Aiee*, the spirit of the country is different," Pale Star observed. "Not unpleasant, but different."

There were two major concerns as they traveled. The first was water. There seemed to be no streams as they knew them, but occasionally a sparkling rivulet tumbled through the reddish rocks to rush on down the slope.

"Will there be water, Turkey Foot?" Sky-Eyes asked. "This is dry country."

"Yes, I think so. There are some places where it is dry for a day's travel. But look, Sky-Eyes. This is a trail that people have traveled. There could not be a trail if the first ones to travel it had not found water, could there?"

This logic seemed sound.

"We have waterskins," their guide continued. "On the dry stretches we carry water."

The other concern was that there was no game. An occasional deer, usually seen at a distance. Sometimes a rabbit. The travelers relied primarily on their dried provisions. There was no time to stop and hunt anyway.

"Do the buffalo come here at all?" Star wondered.

"Not here," Turkey Foot assured. "Farther south there are more open plains. A few there, sometimes."

This young cousin of Lean Bear's seemed to have answers to every question. Either he was skilled and observant, or an expert talker with little real knowledge. Sky-Eyes held some reservation, but so far, it had been as Turkey Foot said. Also, he tried to assure himself, if Lean Bear, who was thoroughly reliable, felt that his cousin was dependable, it should be so. After all, Bear's own life was one of those at risk, too.

Most of the time they seemed to be climbing, Sky-Eyes noticed. There were ups and downs to the trail, as well as windings. Each night they seemed to be a little higher, a little deeper into the mountains. The night air was crisp and cool, and the warmth of their buffalo robes was good.

To the south, when they were able to see for a distance, a heavy line of mountains lay across their path.

"There are plains beyond," assured Turkey Foot. "We cross through these mountains and down the other side."

"Are there tribes living in the mountains?" asked Pale Star.

"Probably," responded Turkey Foot, "but I saw none until beyond the pass."

"Are they hunters?"

"Mostly growers, I think. They are mud-lodge people."

They traveled on, sometimes dry and thirsty for a time between streams. The country changed gradually, giving way to more frequent pines on rockier slopes and in rougher canyons. There were new and different small animals. A creature much like a woodchuck sat on a boulder and whistled curiously at the intruders.

Some things seemed the same anywhere. High overhead, a pair of eagles circled and screamed, exactly as they would at home. Or, a coyote would cry into the night from a high ridge, and its mate would answer from beyond. An eerie sound, but a familiar one, which carried with it the reassurance of something familiar.

They posted a watch each night, trading off partway through the time of darkness. There was never any sign of the unusual, or of any other human.

Then, one night, the sameness of their routine was shattered. Sky-Eyes was on watch. The moon was bright, and he was enjoying the beauty of the night. He listened to the distant coyotes, watched a pair of porcupines shuffle around in their odd courting dance. He wondered how it was possible for the creatures to mate without impaling each other. Strange, he thought, an animal that was dangerous if not impossible to touch without injury. Yet it was possible for it to mate and reproduce, somehow avoiding the sharp quills.

He was still pondering the dilemma of the creature, thanking the fates that gave humankind a soft and smooth skin for sensuality, when the sound came. It was for all the world like a woman's scream. Not just a scream, but a nerve-shattering cry that made his neck-hairs stand up and sent a cold chill down his back. At the very least, the scream must have been drawn from the throat of one under torture or being dismembered.

He could hear the frightened horses stamping and struggling in the little pocket where they had been hobbled, and turned in that direction to see to them. There had been no time yet to try to identify what was happening and deal with it. It was only apparent to him that whatever the nature of the emergency, they could not afford to lose the horses. Survival in these dry southern mountains might depend on the ability to travel.

As he moved toward the horses, a thought began to form in his mind. Someone must be attempting to steal the horses, and had created the scream as a diversion. He must be very careful. Whoever the prowlers were, they had probably already spotted him as the man on watch. At any moment, an arrow might come reaching out of the shadows, searching for his vitals. He crouched low and hurried on.

He had almost reached the tethered horses when the cry came again, closer and louder than before. It seemed to be overhead. He glanced upward. There was a movement on the top of a spire of rock that jutted out of the mountain. He watched for a moment, and nearly decided he was mistaken, that there had been only a play of light and shadow. Then the motion came again, and in the moonlight he could plainly see the outlines of a giant cat. The creature lifted its head and screamed again, the hunting cry that chilled the heart of the listener.

Someone moved up behind him, calling his name softly.

"Star? Do you see it?"

"Yes. It is the real-cat, the long-tailed hunter. It smells the horses."

She held her bow, but the animal was just out of range. Behind them, the campfire blazed up and they heard voices as the others came awake. Lean Bear ran up, clutching his bow.

"A real-cat? Where?"

Sky-Eyes pointed to the rock above, but it was unoccupied now. The great hunting cat was gone.

"The horses?" inquired Lean Bear.

They could still hear stamping and nickers of alarm, and they hurried that way. The shifting forms of the animals could be seen ahead of them, jumping around with the odd gait that only a horse with front-leg hobbles possesses. They moved among the horses, talking softly, reassuring, patting the nervous creatures.

The evaluation did not take long.

"Two are missing!" Pale Star announced.

"We cannot search in the dark," Crow observed.

Sky-Eyes recalled that among the Head Splitters, there was a taboo about the night. Not a fear, exactly, but a belief. The spirit of one killed in the darkness could not find its way to the Other Side, and would wander forever.

The real-cat screamed again in the distance, and a chill again gripped Sky-Eyes. The sound was very suggestive of a lost soul, crying in the darkness.

12

» » »

There was little that they could do but wait for daylight. The remaining horses were nervous and frightened, and it took some time to quiet them. The animals kept rolling white-rimmed eyes and jumping at every sound out in the night. Gradually, they calmed, and began to browse again.

It seemed unlikely that the missing animals had been killed by the cougar. They had been hobbled by tying the front feet together with a short strap. This allowed the grazing animal to take short steps or hops, but not to run or trot. It would have prevented a runaway from going far. Surely they would have heard the sounds of an attack.

The cat had definitely not tried for a kill yet when they saw it on the rock, and they had not heard any commotion since. It seemed that the frightened horses must have simply struggled a little way off into the darkness. They searched the immediate area and called for the animals. Once they thought they heard a distant nicker, but it was not repeated. No one wanted to go out into the dark, not even the Elk-dog warriors who often chose to fight at night. The entire situation was too foreign to their experience. They were unfamiliar with the spirits of the mountain country, and uncertain how to relate to them. The cougar was known to their prairie country, but not common. Usually they were seen only at a distance, and then rarely. There had been something very disconcerting about the sudden screams in the night.

The travelers huddled by the fires until morning, building

a second fire near the horses as a deterrent in case the real-cat returned. They discussed their plight, but were forced to agree that they must discover the fate of the missing horses before they could make any decisions.

It seemed a long time before the stars began to dim and the blackness of the night sky softened to gray in the east. Sun Boy thrust his torch over earth's rim and the warming rays began to dispel both the night's chill and its terror.

They rose and began the search. One horse was found immediately, not a bow shot from camp. It had fallen, apparently in mindless flight, breaking both front legs in a crevice in the rocky slope. Turkey Foot ended the creature's suffering.

No matter how they searched and called, there was no sign of the other horse. It seemed to have vanished. The searchers gathered to discuss their next move. It seemed likely that the horse had broken the hobbles, since it would have been difficult for it to move very far otherwise. Beyond that, its fate was questionable. It could have been killed by the real-cat at some distance from the camp, but there was no evidence.

It was frustrating, the lack of ability to track over the rocks. There were those in the party who were known for better than average tracking ability, but this was strange country, with its different spirits. Not a hoofprint could be found that might have been that of the missing horse.

They did find one print that was fascinating in its implications. Turkey Foot called to the others, who hurried over to look at his find. Lean Bear knelt over the sandy spot and spanned the giant cat track with his outspread hand.

"*Aiee!*" someone whispered softly.

"Could a real-cat carry the horse?" Sky-Eyes wondered aloud.

No one laughed.

"A short distance, maybe," Lean Bear said thoughtfully. "Not far. No, that is not the answer."

"An elk-dog likes to return where he came from," observed Beaver Tooth. "Maybe he took the back trail."

It seemed a likely possibility, but there were many things to think of. The horse might be a day's travel away before they recovered it. That would cost four days' travel, one to search for it, another to return to the camp, and then the two days' travel they had lost by waiting.

"But we need the horse!" protested Sky-Eyes.

Finally, they decided to compromise. They would wait for half the day while Turkey Foot, who had the most mountain experience, took the back trail to search. When he returned, with or without the horse, they would be ready to depart. The time of waiting would be used to repack the furs. Everyone would have to carry a greater load now.

In effect, they now had only one pack horse, unless someone walked. The packs from the other two horses must be divided among the six riders and the remaining pack animal. They could be tied behind the saddles. It would be clumsy and inconvenient, but there was no alternative. They set to work, sorting, repacking, and tying.

Turkey Foot returned, somewhat after midday, without the horse. He had found what appeared to be its hoofprints on the back trail, and followed it for some distance. He had been tempted, he reported, to pursue it farther, but knew the others were waiting. Besides, the trail he was following was becoming no fresher.

"*Aiee,*" he exclaimed, "the horse was going home. I might not have caught up until he reached our village!"

The trail indicated that the horse was moving fairly rapidly. It was to be assumed that it had broken the hobble, or that the knots had come untied. They loaded quickly and moved on.

They had learned one thing for certain, however, by the end of the day. They would not be able to carry the divided packs in this way. The bundles kept slipping, sliding around, coming loose, even falling to the ground. At one point, Crow's pack loosened at one side. The other end slid across the horse's rump, startling it into a bucking fit for a hundred paces down the trail. Crow clung like a burr to the horse's back, but was finally dislodged to land hard beside the trail. Furs were scattered down the slope.

"Let us camp here," suggested Pale Star. "We have to repack anyway."

"Yes," agreed Turkey Foot, "but we should go a little farther. I think there is a spring just a little way ahead."

He moved ahead and found the area he remembered, while others gathered the spilled furs.

They saw no more of the real-cat. However, they carefully posted an extra watch, and kept fires burning, not only at the camp but near the place where the horses were hobbled. It was not a restful night.

13

» » »

The most pressing problem as they prepared to move out next morning was that of how to rearrange the packs. They could trade off, with four people riding, the others walking, and their horses carrying packs. It seemed, however, that this would be impractical. If the two halves of the party were traveling at different speeds, they must either split up or travel at the slowest speed of any of those on foot.

They did not know how important speed might be. They had little knowledge of when winter might come to these southern mountains. The nights were cool, though, and none of the travelers wanted to be caught unprepared.

Reluctantly, they came to a decision. They would have to abandon a portion of their trade goods. They considered sending one or two men back with part of the furs, but the same problem arose. That would not in any way help the shortage of horses, unless those turning back walked. It was this unacceptable solution that finally decided their course. For a warrior of the plains, his horse was all-important. It was a matter of prestige, as well as practical necessity, and a man unhorsed was somehow less of a man.

There was reason behind this. To be on foot in the far-flung country of the New World could be dangerous. Distances were great, and it was often far between sources of water and food. There was always some threat from wild animals. In addition, in this case, they were in unfamiliar country. No one except Turkey Foot had ever been here before. They had very little knowledge of what tribes they might encounter, or whether they would be friendly or hostile. No, they must stay together, and remain mounted. The pack horse would carry as much as was practical, and then each individual would carry a small bundle of furs.

Once more, the packs were opened and sorted. It was their goal now to take only examples of the best, along with a robe or two.

"What shall we do with the rest?" Lean Bear voiced the question.

"Could we pack them and hide them here?" suggested Pale Star. "The tribes farther north do this with supplies. It is called a *cache*."

Sky-Eyes nodded.

"That is a word from my tribe," he agreed. "A place for storage."

They scattered along the slope, searching for a suitable hiding place, protected from the weather. There was a rocky shelf whose overhanging lip seemed to offer what they sought. The packs would be protected from the rain here, and not easily visible from the trail. They dug back into the soft shale a little way, making a hole in which to place the bundles. Then they placed a few larger stones in front, and scattered loose shale to complete the camouflage. They carefully obliterated footprints and other signs of activity as they backed away.

"A *cache* is usually honored by anyone who finds it, and left alone," Pale Star commented.

"But we do not know the tribes in this place, or who might travel the trail," Sky-Eyes stated. "Well, if we lose it, so be it. We tried."

There was a brief discussion as to whether they should cut a few pieces of brush for further camouflage.

"Of course not," laughed Turkey Foot. "In this country, everyone is looking for dead brush to burn for fuel. That would call attention to it."

"How will we find it again?" someone asked.

It was quite invisible from the trail. Finally, it was discovered that as one walked or rode along the path, an odd-shaped knob of stone caught the eye. It was perhaps two bow shots off the trail, and well beyond the *cache*. When the observer moved until the rock (shaped like a bear's head) was exactly in line with a distant snowcapped peak, it was also in line with the hiding place.

"Now, any of us can find the *cache* if we need to," Sky-Eyes announced.

Unspoken was the rest of that thought. They were probing farther and farther into the unknown. There would be danger, and it was quite possible that they would not all survive this venture. The unspoken part of Sky-Eyes' statement was that any *survivor* could salvage their hidden goods.

They had seen no sign of any inhabitants of the area. There had been no human contact, in fact, since they left the Red Rocks several sleeps before. Sky-Eyes asked Turkey Foot about it.

"Are there people in this area?"

"Not many, I think, Sky-Eyes. We saw villages, but not until after we crossed the pass."

"And they do not use the hand-sign talk?"

"Some, not much. Most of them know some of the Hairface tongue."

Sky-Eyes had been somewhat concerned about how they would communicate, and it was reassuring to learn that there was some use of Spanish. Pale Star had assured him that language was no problem to a trader.

"Look, you hold an item and point, offering to exchange for something they have. I will show you. It will be no problem."

That was very well for her to say, he thought. Star was fluent in French and in several native tongues, from her days with the traveling trader and his wife. He felt that, even as a captive, she had learned to enjoy the excitement of the trading. This venture stirred the old excitement.

He wondered how long it would take for her to acquire a working knowledge of trader Spanish. Not long, he suspected. He had seen her in action when they had encountered river tribes on their journey back to her people. She could communicate with anyone, he suspected, with facial expression, gestures, sign-talk, or in the variety of tongues she had encountered. It was a strange thing, he pondered that night, snuggling close to her warm body under their buffalo robe. Why was it that some people seemed to have this gift of communication, the ability to talk to those of other cultures? His own skill with language was moderately good, but there was no comparison to Star's.

"What is it, my husband?" she whispered in the darkness. "You are still awake."

"It is nothing. I was only thinking about the trading."

"I, too," she chuckled, the delightful little laugh that he had always loved, like the ripple of water over white gravel.

"Your heart is good for this venture."

It was a statement, not a question.

"Yes," she answered slowly. "You would have to understand the trading, Sky-Eyes. There is excitement, and joy, and the unexpected. It is much like wondering what is over the next hill."

"And you have not had a chance to trade for many seasons. Not since I have known you!"

"Only the trading with the Growers for corn and beans and pumpkins."

"The stories?" he asked.

Star was a renowned storyteller. She could captivate an audience, even in sign-talk. She had encouraged him to tell stories, too, and he had enjoyed it. He had wondered what his professors would have said, if they had known that their former student was telling stories of the Trojan War in sign-talk to natives in the New World.

"The stories are part of it, Sky-Eyes," she assured him. "You get to know people at the story fires, and they come to trust you because they know you. Then, the trading is better the next day."

She was silent a long time.

"I wish Traveler and Plum Leaf were with us," she said softly. "Traveler's heart would be very glad for this."

14

» » »

"**W**hat do the Hairfaces do?" Sky-Eyes asked their guide one morning as they traveled.

"What do you mean, Sky-Eyes?"

"Well, what are they doing at this Santa Fe? Do they grow corn, or hunt, or fish?"

"No, no. Well, there is some corn. They have some spotted buffalo, which they eat sometimes."

There was a moment of confusion while they looked for a word to express "cattle." Well, Sky-Eyes concluded, "spotted buffalo" would do. There was little doubt that Turkey Foot was referring to cattle.

"Sometimes they tie the spotted buffalo to a pole-drag with round shields on the sides," he continued. "They pull loads."

"Yes, ox-carts."

"There are other animals that they eat, too, and use the skins."

"What animals? Elk-dogs?"

"No, no, smaller animals, like a little deer, with fur like a buffalo. All colors."

Sheep, Sky-Eyes thought.

"What else?"

"Many warriors. They walk around in straight lines sometimes. They have many chiefs, who stay in a big lodge."

"A mud-lodge?"

"Yes, of course. It is maybe a hundred paces long."

Sky-Eyes pondered. A building that large, even allowing

53

for exaggeration by Turkey Foot, must be an official government building of some sort. What was this Santa Fe?

"Oh yes," Turkey Foot continued, "they eat birds, too."

"Birds?"

"Yes, they keep them in cages, or sometimes they run loose, but they do not fly away. The Hairfaces eat their eggs."

So, the Spanish were well established here, apparently with regular supply lines, or at least, self-sufficient. They were raising cattle, sheep, and poultry. A thought made him ask another question.

"Are these birds like ducks?"

"No. They don't go in the water. Like this."

Turkey Foot raised his elbows, flapped them, and crowed like a rooster. There was no mistaking his action.

Chickens, Sky-Eyes thought. Again, there came the problem with a word that would be meaningful to both.

"These are like a sharp-nosed duck with turkey feet?"

Turkey Foot laughed.

"Yes, maybe so. Like a little turkey, with a red headdress."

He held his fingers over his head, pointing upward like the bird's comb.

Apparently, this settlement had been there for some time, and was a seat of provincial government of some sort. And the "many warriors" Turkey Foot described? How many men were stationed there? A platoon of uniformed soldiers might appear to be a great number to the young warrior.

"Turkey Foot," he asked, "how many warriors did you see?"

"Many."

"How were they dressed?"

"Blue coats, blue leggings. A headdress and a white sash." He indicated the uniform sash around the waist.

"What are their weapons?"

"Some carry buffalo spears. Others long knives."

Turkey Foot extended his hands to show the length of the weapon, obviously a saber.

"Do all of the warriors ride elk-dogs?"

"Most of them. Some walk and carry thunder-sticks."

"And they were many?"

"Yes, Uncle. About this many."

He resorted to sign-talk to express how many, making the sign for ten with fingers spread, followed by touching his right little finger with his left index finger. Ten, times ten. This was easier than learning to count in each other's languages.

About a hundred, then, thought Sky-Eyes. Lancers, dragoons, and even a squad of musketeers. A real show of force. He wondered if the English and Spanish were still at war. For that matter, he did not even know whether the English and French were still at war. The political problems of Europe seemed distant and unimportant, here among the People and their allies.

But, if Spain had stationed many troops in the New World, there might be recent developments since his last contact with civilization. That was five years ago now, through the return of Sergeant Cartier, now Woodchuck. There had been no such news at that time, but the French were beginning to explore the great river system of the middle of the continent. It had been such an exploration, in fact, that had enabled Woodchuck to return to the People.

Ah, well, they would learn in due time. First, they must reach Santa Fe. He smiled to himself at his own attitude. There was still some of his youthful impatience in evidence, but it had moderated considerably. The easy, day-at-a-time way of the People was contagious. The days of travel were not unpleasant, in the clear sunlight of the mountain air. Neither were the crisp cool nights.

Then came the day when they rounded the shoulder of a rocky hillside and Turkey Foot pointed ahead. In the distance appeared a notch or cleft in the line of mountains to the south.

"The pass," he said simply.

The smile of success on his face was as proud as if he had carved the pass himself, out of the solid rock.

"Does it have a name?" asked Sky-Eyes.

"Yes, 'Raton,'" the young man answered. "We cross the ridge there and move on south and west."

"How far to the pass?"

Turkey Foot shrugged.

"Maybe two, three sleeps."

"It looks much closer."

"Yes. That is a trick of the eyes."

From time to time there was no glimpse at all of the pass. Then again, they would be able to watch it as they traveled, beckoning them to hurry. And each view was different. The effects of light and shadow on the colors of the distant mountains were always changing. In the distance, the effects ranged from blue to an assortment of purples.

From a closer vantage point, the red-brown of the rocks and the green of the pines and juniper made an interesting mosaic, still changing with light and shadow. In the mornings, the direct sun brightened the colors and intensified the contrasts as it burned away the wisps of mist in the canyons.

Most spectacular, though, was the splendor of the setting sun as it dipped below the mountains to the west. A long north-south range stretched as far as the eye could see in both directions. It was behind this that the setting sun sank to end each day. There would be a few moments before dark when the entire range would seem to be splashed with crimson on each peak.

Sky-Eyes was watching the spectacle one evening when his wife came up behind him and slipped an arm around his waist.

"It is beautiful, my husband. Sun Boy has splashed the mountains with his paint."

They stood watching while the colors changed from fiery orange to deeper scarlet, and finally blood-red.

"It is as red as blood," Star murmured.

It would be some time before they learned that the Spanish had observed the same phenomenon. Their name for this range would remain in use for centuries: *Sangre de Cristo*— "the Blood of Christ."

For the present, Sky-Eyes was only hoping that the blood-red sunset was not an unfavorable omen.

15

» » »

The travelers stood at the pass and looked southward across the plain. The flat but slightly rolling country stretched to the south and east as far as eye could see. It was a relief, of sorts, for these people of the prairie. Their days of mountain trails had become irritating to them. Accustomed to far horizons, they had had great difficulty adjusting to the sensation of looming masses of rock above their line of vision as they traveled.

Now, they could see for vast distances again, to where the earth met the sky.

"Aiee!" exclaimed Pale Star. "Earth's rim!"

They all laughed, and the tension was broken. Sky-Eyes had not realized the extent to which this closed-in feeling had affected him.

"You knew of this feeling?" he asked his wife.

"Not really. I have felt it before. Mountains or forests are not for people of the prairie. Their spirit is different."

"Spirit? The spirit of the mountains or of the people?"

"Both!" she smiled. "The spirit of anyone must rest comfortably with the spirit of a place. It can be learned, as you and Woodchuck have done, or it may be something we are born with."

"Like you."

"Yes."

She was self-conscious now.

"When I was a prisoner with the Forest People, I used to

57

dream. I longed to see earth's rim, and the sky. You feel it, too, I know you do."

"Yes," he admitted, "but I did not know what it was. Do all people feel this way?"

"I think not, Sky-Eyes. Only people of the grassland, and some more than others. But of course," she added with a smile, "people of the woods or mountains would feel lost in our grassland. They would want part of the sky covered with trees or rocks. It is a thing of the spirits."

He nodded, not quite understanding. Even after his years with the People, he was not quite secure in the idea of a place or an area possessing a spirit.

"But Sky-Eyes," Star had once said, "all things have spirits."

He had to admit that, from a practical point of view, it was a workable philosophy. It was a different "feel" in different locales. And, he must admit, the view of a rolling plain, even a strange one, made him feel more at home than he had for some time. Yes, he had become a man of the prairie, of the big sky and the far horizons.

The travelers stood, not ready yet to start down the other side.

"The colors are different," observed Star.

It was true. Such a vista in the Tallgrass Hills, for instance, would have been in shades of blue and green in summer, with distant slopes more bluish until the farthest range was nearly the color of the sky. In autumn, greens would have been replaced by orange and pink as the ripe grasses assumed their winter coloration.

Here, the tones were of reddish brown, like the stones of the mountain slopes. In the distance, the hues faded to muted purples, with gray-green or tawny patches of vegetation. An eagle circled high overhead, and Sky-Eyes wondered at all that the bird might see. Mountains to the north and west, plains to the south and east. What would it look like from up there, he wondered.

The sun was lowering in the west now, and there was a hint of evening chill in the breeze that floated up the southern slope to meet them. They had noticed this quality in the higher altitudes of recent days.

In the Tallgrass Hills, this was still the Red Moon, August by the count of his own culture, Sky-Eyes believed. The days would be uncomfortably warm sometimes, but the nights more acceptable. Here in the mountains, on the other hand, though the days were warm, temperatures at night often became almost miserable. The bone-chilling cold seemed to soak through one's body, and it took until mid-morning to warm fingers and toes. Sky-Eyes was glad for the comfort of Star's warm body next to his as they sought their robes each night.

"We must find a spot to camp," Turkey Foot observed, adjusting his pack.

"Is there water ahead?" asked his cousin.

"Yes, but I have forgotten where. It is on the trail."

The trail was still plain, sometimes meandering like the game trail that was its origin, sometimes clearly trodden by many generations of moccasined feet. Of one thing they could be certain. If others had traveled this way, there must have been water. They had only to stay on the same course followed previously.

Still, it was nearly night before they found the spring, tucked in against the mountain's steep face. Quickly, they scattered to gather fuel before darkness closed in.

The campsite was well located, sheltered from the main thrust of the wind. In a short while, the horses were picketed, and the aromatic smoke of dry piñon rose from the camp fire. Lean Bear tucked his fire-making sticks away and rose to see to the other minor chores that had to do with the preparation for the night. The expanding light from the fire crowded shadows back into the rocks and scrub junipers. The travelers began to gather at the fire, warming themselves as they spread robes, and chewing bites of dried meat.

"*Aiee*, the fire feels good!" Star observed.

"Yes," agreed Lean Bear. "The spirit of this place is good!"

Its spirit. Yes, Sky-Eyes had noticed before, there were favorite camping places in the country of the People. It was not that the water or the grass were so favorable, though those could be factors, too. Most campsites had been used for generations, the fires built sometimes upon the ashes of other fires long dead. Why was one site more favored than another? There was simply a *feel* about a place that made it more comfortable. Its *spirit* was right.

Squatting here before this crackling fire, with Star at his elbow, he had the feeling that the spirit of this place had been good for many people. He saw a smudge of soot against an overhanging red rock. Someone had built a fire there, some time long ago. There were no traces of ashes or partly burned charcoal in evidence. They had long since weathered away. He wondered about the traveler who had stopped here for the night, to squat by a fire maybe generations ago. Where was the man from, and where was he going? Did he have hopes and dreams, and did he laugh at jokes around the story-fires? Did he make love, and raise a family? Was he alone when he stopped here, or was he part of a hunting party or even a war party?

Turkey Foot rose from the fire, shook out his robe, and spread it to roll in a little distance away.

"We will probably see some of the mud-lodge people tomorrow," he said casually.

16
» » »

Their first contact was not the following day, but several days later. When they came to the first of the mud-lodge towns, it was something of a surprise. They had come through a section of broken foothills and rounded the shoulder of a ridge to see the village lying directly before them. It was no more than a few bow shots away. The travelers stopped to look for a moment.

There was not much difference, thought Sky-Eyes, between this cluster of dwellings and those of Southern France or Spain. He had spent some time in that area, long ago when he was André Du Pres. The major difference that these lodges lacked the thatched roofs, and were flat on the top. They were also clustered closely together, sometimes seeming to have a wall in common with the next structure.

To his surprise, he saw that some dwellings were actually placed one on top of the other, like a child's play blocks. The steps could be plainly seen, clinging to the side of the outside wall.

Doors and windows showed darkly in contrast to the uniform pinkish-beige earth tones that gave a pervading color to the scene. Actually, Sky-Eyes felt, the whole effect was that of sameness of color. At this point the world seemed all the same neutral hue. It would have been easy, he thought, to pass by at a little distance without even noticing that a village stood there. The mud-lodges, made of the earth itself, were of the same color, and blended into the sameness of their origin. A departure from the soft color of the earth was that of the dark window-openings, and a few specks of green on the hills. All cedars and juniper in the immediate area had long ago been used as fuel, he suspected.

As if to contradict his observations, a gigantic cottonwood tree towered over the cluster of dwellings. Apparently taking its sustenance from the small stream that flowed past the village, the lone giant stood protectingly overhead, like a massive umbrella.

A few people were seen moving among the dwellings. In a flat area near the village several worked together. At first it was puzzling, what they were doing. Then Sky-Eyes realized that this was the process by which the mud bricks were made. He recalled the Spanish word, used for both the process and the product. *Adobe.* In a shallow depression, people trod rhythmically, the muddy mixture splashing as high as their knees. It reminded him of the festivities surrounding the grape harvest.

Nearby, other people were packing the muddy mix into rectangles to dry. A stack of drying bricks showed completion of the finished building material. Just now, as they approached, a man was dumping a basket of chopped hay or dried grass into the pit. For some reason, the memory of Sky-Eyes roved back to his instruction as a child, and his mother's interpretation of a biblical story. The Israelites were forced to make bricks for the Pharaoh. As some sort of punishment, he recalled, they were made to gather the straw which was mixed into the bricks, but allowed no time in which to do it. It had been difficult for him to understand this problem, the straw and the bricks. Now, a lifetime later, and on the other side of the world, he was watching the process. It gave him a strange feeling, like stepping back in time.

Curious eyes watched as they passed. It was obvious that these newcomers were people of another culture, a strange and alien race, to the inhabitants of the village.

Dogs ran to bark at the little caravan, but not in the numbers that would be present in one of the camps of the People. On a slope beyond the village, scattered sheep browsed among the brush.

"Look, Sky-Eyes! There are the birds I told you of!" exclaimed Turkey Foot.

A few chickens scratched in the dust beside one of the dwellings. These people had certainly adopted the ways of the Spanish in some respects, Sky-Eyes noted.

"What should we do now?" he asked.

Turkey Foot shrugged.

"I do not know. We can stop in some place near the lodges, and wait."

There seemed to be an open area of public use, and they moved in that direction, pausing to water the horses as they crossed the stream. People still eyed them with open curiosity, but paid little attention otherwise. They stopped in the open place and dismounted. A woman was taking bread from a mud oven, and the breeze brought a whiff of a delectable aroma. They stood and waited, unsure how to proceed.

"Look! Someone comes," observed Pale Star.

Three men were walking toward them. One carried a bow, but it seemed plain that the people of this village neither meant harm nor feared it. They stopped expectantly, and the man in the middle spoke a few words, in a completely unintelligible tongue.

"Can you understand him, Turkey Foot?" Sky-Eyes asked.

"Not I."

Sky-Eyes looked around him at the blank looks on the faces of the others of his party.

"*Ah-koh,*" he spoke, giving at the same time the hand-sign for greeting.

"I am Sky-Eyes, of the Elk-dog People," he continued in hand-signs.

There were only looks of nonunderstanding on the part of the villagers. The leader shook his head. These people seemed completely unfamiliar with sign-talk.

"How did you talk with them before?" he asked Turkey Foot.

"I did not, Sky-Eyes. Someone in the party spoke in some tongue they understood."

An idea occurred to him.

"*Habla español?*" he asked.

The reaction was unexpected. Expressions of friendly curiosity changed to suspicion.

"Who are you? Spanish?" the leader asked in Spanish, answering the question without a direct response.

"No. We are from beyond the mountains. We are called Elk-dog People."

He thought it just as well not to mention that two of their companions were of a tribe called Head Splitters.

"Then how do you know Spanish?"

The man was not convinced.

"I learned it as a child," Sky-Eyes said truthfully.

"What do you want here?"

"We wish to trade." He pointed to the packs. "We would trade furs and robes to the Spanish for medicine knives and arrow points."

He indicated the knife at his waist.

"Yes," the man said cautiously. "There is much of the Spanish that is useful."

"I am called Sky-Eyes. How are you called?"

The other seemed to relax somewhat. He smiled.

"I am Blue Corn," he offered. "Your people are welcome at our pueblo."

The sun was low, and they must find a place to camp and food for the horses.

"Good. Thank you. May we camp over there? We can talk later."

"Of course. My house is that one," he pointed. "You will eat with me?"

"Thank you, my chief. We will be pleased."

17

» » »

"**I**t would be well to give Blue Corn a gift," observed Pale Star as they hobbled the horses.

"What should we offer?" Sky-Eyes asked.

"I do not know. Something they would not have, if we can."

"A robe?"

"Maybe. But we have few robes."

She turned to Turkey Foot.

"What furs do we have that are scarce here?"

He shrugged.

"They are much the same, I suppose. Fewer buffalo. Otter, maybe?"

"Yes!" exclaimed Sky-Eyes. "Even if they have otter, they would be fewer, because of the smaller streams here. Besides, we use otter skins for ceremonies . . . medicine. They will understand such a gift."

They opened one of the smaller packs and carefully selected a prime otter skin. The thick glossy fur fairly shone in the light of the setting sun. Sky-Eyes stroked the supple softness appreciatively. It was a tanned skin, one of the finest quality, such as a person might sacrifice at the Sun Dance.

"This should do well," he told the others. "I will tell him of its medicine."

They finished establishing their camp, placing a few sticks of firewood to indicate where a camp fire should be. Sky-

Eyes was mildly amused at the fire ritual. The lighting of a fire was almost a sacred act at a new camp, even a temporary one. It seemed somehow to represent a formal communication with the place. In this case, they did not even intend to light a fire, at least for the present. Still, without question, the travelers placed sticks of fuel to mark the place where the fire would dwell. It was like a public announcement to whatever spirits might inhabit the area. "Here we intend to camp."

He recalled an event in his native France, a ritual lighting of the first fire in a new house. Perhaps this was much the same, but transposed to another land and changed to fit the culture of the nomadic People. Maybe it did make sense. In Europe, it had been a matter of bringing good luck. Here, it was a communication with the spirits. Was it the same thing? Whatever, he felt closer to the spirits of the land since he had become a man of the People. Perhaps the medicine of the fire made the difference.

They washed at the stream, and made their way to the lodge of Blue Corn, who greeted them with a smile.

"Come in! Welcome to my lodge," he spoke in Spanish.

The people of the open prairie entered with a tiny bit of uneasiness. Even Sky-Eyes had become so acclimated to the feeling of far horizons that he felt closed in, in a massive structure of this sort. It was similar to the reluctance of the People to enter the half-underground lodges of the Growers. Some could hardly stand the feeling of confinement.

This lodge, they found, was not so threatening. It helped somewhat that the structure was larger, and that it had window openings. In a little while they became accustomed to the feeling and were able to relax a bit.

They sat, and waited a moment for their eyes to accommodate to the dusky room. A fireplace in one corner shed a flickering gleam which augmented the dying light of the day. Long garlands of dried corn, onions, and bright red peppers festooned the poles that formed the ceiling. There was a mix of unfamiliar odors that told of food preparation. A girl of perhaps ten summers assisted an older woman, bringing something hot from the mud oven outside to be used at the work area on the hearth.

"Tell me of your country," Blue Corn was saying.

"Of course, my chief," Sky-Eyes answered, "but first, we wish to give you this small gift."

He drew the otter skin from his robe and presented it. The eyes of Blue Corn grew wide as he stroked the pelt.

"What is it?"

"I do not know your word, or that in Spanish. It lives in the water. Eats fish."

"Ah yes," nodded the other. "I do not know the word, either, but I know of these animals. I have seen their furs, but none of this beauty!"

"Our people use this fur for things of medicine," Sky-Eyes explained. "Pouches, or to decorate the medicine pipe."

"Yes. It appears to have strong medicine," Blue Corn observed. "I will regard it highly."

Sky-Eyes paused to translate the exchange for the others. It was a strange turn of events to find himself acting as interpreter, using a tongue not his own, between people who spoke three other tongues, none of which was his own. Then he turned back to their host.

"You have asked of our country, my chief. We live far to the east, and hunt the buffalo. There are no mountains, only low hills covered with grass."

"Your people raise corn?"

"No, we grow no crops. We only hunt."

Blue Corn's mouth dropped open in astonishment.

"But can you live in that way?"

"Yes, there are many buffalo. We trade robes and meat for corn and beans and pumpkins."

"Then there are those who grow?"

"Yes, the Growers. We trade with them."

"Ah yes. I have heard of hunters such as you. What manner of lodges do you build?"

Sky-Eyes searched for a moment for a word for "tents," and could not find one.

"Skin shelters," he said, "like this."

He held his hands like a pointed lodge.

"We move our lodges when we travel," he finished.

"Yes, I had heard of this," agreed Blue Corn. "I had forgotten."

"Tell me," asked Sky-Eyes curiously, "we have been told of lodges such as yours, *adobe*, with no doors, where the people go in and out the smokehole. Is this true?"

The other man laughed.

"Yes, some of the pueblo people used to do this. They would climb a pole with notches, to the roof, and then pull up the pole and use it to go down through a hole. It is used but little anymore. Most of our people use doors, like this."

"They got that from the Spanish?"

"No, we used some doors before. Mostly inside. I do not know. Customs change."

"It is no matter. I only wondered. Now, can you tell us of the Spanish?"

"Yes, but now the food is ready. Let us eat."

The woman, whom Blue Corn now introduced as his wife, passed steaming bowls of stewed corn and beans to the guests. There were also chunks of meat, and thin flat cakes of ground corn from the oven, to be used as bread. The food was good, with exotic unfamiliar herbs and spices. Lean Bear appeared suspicious at first, but was soon eating eagerly. Sky-Eyes was not surprised. He had seen Lean Bear eat before, and nothing seemed to affect the young man's appetite. Pale Star, with gastronomic experience in many tribes, was thoroughly enjoying the new tastes.

When the meal was finished and the utensils cleared away, they brought out the pipes, to smoke and talk. Conversation continued until far into the night, with Sky-Eyes translating. They exchanged creation stories, laughed and joked and passed the pipe, and at last discussed the Spanish.

"There are good Spanish and bad, Sky-Eyes, like any other people," observed their host. "You will be careful?"

"Of course, my friend. Is there a way to tell the good from the bad?"

Both laughed, but then Blue Corn became serious.

"I think the way to tell is to trust no one, and then see which ones try to do you evil."

They returned to their fireless camp, and prepared to seek their robes. Lean Bear kindled a token fire to complete the ritual, though it was unneeded and would soon die.

Sky-Eyes and Pale Star snuggled together against the cold,

under the warmth of the buffalo robes. She was silent a long time, and he thought she was asleep, but finally she spoke softly.

"Sky-Eyes?"

"Yes. What is it?"

"Sky-Eyes, I think I must learn the tongue of the Spanish."

18

》》》

Several days later, they encountered their first Spaniards. They had seen another pueblo, and camped nearby, but did not make the prolonged close contact that they had previously with their pueblo host. They had inquired more about the trail to Santa Fe, and the villages and tribes they might encounter. Blue Corn had instructed them in great detail.

"I will look for you on the return trip," he had offered.

"It is good. We will stop here," Sky-Eyes had assured him.

Their encounter with the Spanish was totally without warning. The little caravan topped a rise to see a mounted patrol approaching, perhaps two bow shots away. Sky-Eyes held up a hand to signal a halt, and waited for the horsemen to approach.

He evaluated the patrol quickly. Soldiers, under command of a very young lieutenant. The grizzled old sergeant at the officer's left would be the man with experience, he judged. The others were the usual run of colonial troops, seven lancers in all. The Spaniards seemed arrogant, somewhat interested, and not particularly hostile.

Now Sky-Eyes found himself in a peculiarly strange position. He, as a French officer, would have been the equal in every way of this unit's commander. Yet he dare not reveal his French identity. The two countries might easily be at war, since they frequently were. He could be imprisoned. They all might be, anyway, he realized. For a moment the whole idea of this trading expedition seemed sheer idiocy.

What were they doing here in an unknown country with its dangers?

The patrol now approached and halted, and the lieutenant kneed his horse forward a little, the sergeant at his elbow. Behind the two, the lancers relaxed a little, and Sky-Eyes caught a scrap of their conversation.

"Mother of God!" exclaimed one trooper. "Look at the woman. That would warm a man's bed!"

The others chuckled. Anger rose in Sky-Eyes' throat. This was a situation he had not foreseen. Should he pretend that he did not understand the talk of the soldiers? By rights, their officer should have better discipline. Certainly, troops under his own command would not have behaved in this manner.

Then the facts struck him. The Spanish reputation for treatment of natives, anywhere, was not the best. Even the English had traditionally used some tribes as allies, but Spain had dominated, in some cases even enslaved or killed entire tribes, he had heard. He experienced a chill of fear. What was to prevent this officer from ordering their entire party killed, and confiscating their goods?

"Silence!" the lieutenant suddenly snapped over his shoulder.

Sky-Eyes relaxed a trifle. That was the proper action for a military officer.

"Thank you, lieutenant," he spoke tersely. "The woman they speak of so freely is my wife!"

The lieutenant's eyes widened, as he tried to maintain his composure.

"Who are you?" he snapped.

"I am Sky-Eyes, of the Elk-dog People."

"Elk-dog? The 'Horse People'?"

"Yes. So we are called. We call ourselves only 'the People.'"

"I do not know your tribe."

"Our country is far to the east."

The lieutenant was plainly curious.

"How is it that you speak Spanish?"

Somehow, Sky-Eyes had not foreseen this interrogation.

At least not so probing a conversation. He tried to remain calm, and shrugged nonchalantly.

"I learned it as a child."

"From whom?" the lieutenant probed.

"I do not remember. There were those who spoke your tongue."

This questioning was beginning to irritate Sky-Eyes.

"Look," the lieutenant persisted, "you are called Sky-Eyes? But the others, here, do not have eyes like yours. Is this common in your tribe?"

"Of course not! If all the People had eyes of blue, I would not have such a name. It would mean nothing."

"But how are yours blue? How are you different?"

This line of questioning was insolent, and Sky-Eyes resented it. He tried to tell himself that the young officer was only doing his job. It was a new experience to be questioned in this manner. But, at all costs, he must avoid antagonizing the soldiers. These were the people with whom they hoped to trade. He tried to remain calm and relaxed, shrugging as if it did not matter.

"My father had blue eyes," he stated calmly.

"You are a half-breed?"

The question irritated Sky-Eyes more than any of the probing so far. For the first time he felt the stigma of accusation, the mark of being labeled less than a human being. It was not that he wished to deny the appellation. His son would bear that distinction, and Sky-Eyes hoped that the boy would be proud of his heritage.

To further confuse his thinking, they might be treated with more respect if Sky-Eyes admitted his French background. Or with less, if the French and Spanish were at war. No, he must appear to be what he felt himself to be, and speak as near the truth as possible.

"My father was a hairface," he spoke with dignity, "like him." He pointed to the grizzled sergeant. "I am a warrior of the People."

The lieutenant seemed satisfied that he had the answer to that question, and shifted to another line of inquiry.

"What are you doing here?"

Sky-Eyes was relieved by the change of direction in the conversation.

"We seek to trade."

He turned and spoke to Pale Star, who came forward to hand him a previously selected pelt. Sky-Eyes ceremoniously presented it to the lieutenant.

"A small gift for you, Captain," Sky-Eyes offered, consciously giving the young officer a rank above his actual commission. "We can bring many such skins to trade."

This portion of the meeting was carefully calculated. Sky-Eyes was familiar with the process of "greasing the palm with silver" to accomplish a thing. By winning the cooperation of the officer, they would have a contact among the Spanish.

The lieutenant thoughtfully stroked the soft fur with his thumb. He had apparently decided to overlook his sudden promotion to Captain.

"You go to Santa Fe?"

"Unless there is some better place to go."

"What do you wish in trade?"

"Iron tools. Knives, arrow points, lance heads."

He very nearly pointed to the medicine knife at his waist, but a warning thought struck him. This Spanish officer would have little trouble recognizing the weapon's French pattern. *Aiee*, this was a complicated business!

"Is your lodge at Santa Fe?" Sky-Eyes asked.

He had almost asked "is your unit stationed at Santa Fe?" but caught himself in time.

"Yes," the lieutenant answered. "We will return there in three days."

"How far is it?"

"You will reach it tomorrow."

"It is good," said Sky-Eyes solemnly.

"You do not carry much goods," observed the lieutenant, pointing to the pack horse.

"We lost a horse," Sky-Eyes explained. "We decided to bring only samples to show, to see if we could come back with more."

The officer nodded.

"It is a good plan. When you reach Santa Fe, ask for Captain Martínez. Tell him you have spoken with me, Lieutenant Díaz. He will help you."

"It is good," answered Sky-Eyes. "We will do so."

They parted, and Sky-Eyes quickly related the conversation to the others.

"Do you think he can be trusted?" asked Lean Bear.

"I do not know. But I think we know one thing. Captain Martínez is trusted by this young chief. So, either both are honest, or both cannot be trusted. We will see which."

19

》 》 》

Lieutenant Díaz pondered at great length as he rode. It had been quite a surprise to encounter the party of would-be traders on the trail. These were natives from a tribe he had never met before. One from the far grasslands, he supposed. Horse People, they had said they were called. Well, if the animals they rode were any indication, the name was well deserved. He had noted one gray mare that appeared to be of finest Andalusian stock.

There had been natives, from time to time, seeking to trade in Santa Fe. It was not too unusual. These people, however, seemed of different racial stock. Even discounting their leader, the blue-eyed half-breed who spoke Spanish, these travelers were of a different body type than the local natives. They were long-legged, tall, and the structure of their facial bones was somewhat different. The faces were long ovals, with strong noses and high cheekbones, unlike the roundfaced tribes of the area. He had seen some natives of similar type, but had not noticed the contrast to this extent.

Perhaps it was the striking appearance of the woman. Mother of God, what a beauty! He wondered if all of the women of the Elk-dog People were so endowed. Her finely chiseled features were like those of a Roman goddess. Her gracefully shaped body seemed created to be looked at and appreciated by men. She sat a horse like a soldier, her back ramrod-straight. It was no wonder that his lancers had expressed their appreciation in ribald remarks.

The most striking quality of the woman's appearance, however, was not her obvious beauty. There was something about the fire in her eye, a look like that in the eye of a fine hot-blood horse, or the eye of an eagle. Yes, that was it, like the look of eagles. Not defiance, exactly, but confidence, self-assurance. This was no woman to be trifled with.

And what of her man, the blue-eyed one who had done the talking? He had been angered for a moment at the vulgar remarks of the lancers. The man had been in no position to protest, but had done so anyway. This was a man who was accustomed to having his orders obeyed without question. He had been playing a part, so to speak.

There was much that Díaz did not understand here, things that did not quite add up. The story of being "Elk-dog People" seemed to be reliable. The quality of their horses seemed to support such a name. The animals were also well conditioned and well trained, and their riders seemed to manage them well. All the tribes now had access to horses, and this tribe had undoubtedly chanced to acquire some good blooded stock, and somehow learned to manage the animals to best advantage. That could be explained.

But what about the blue-eyed man, the husband of the strikingly beautiful woman? They appeared about the same age, perhaps thirty. In fact, the others in the party seemed all of this age, some perhaps a bit younger. The blue-eyed man acted as their leader, but had not referred to himself as a "chief," which might have been expected. He admitted to being a half-breed. Well, that was quite possible. There had been several Spanish expeditions into the plains over the last century.

The most puzzling thing about the man was not his air of authority, or even his light-colored eyes. There were light-eyed soldiers among the troops, usually those from northern Spain. Díaz had no doubt that such a soldier had sired the mysterious half-breed who called himself Sky-Eyes. The great mystery, however, was the man's fluent use of Spanish. If he had been born as the result of a chance liaison, his father would have moved on. There would have been no way for this Sky-Eyes to have learned the tongue of his father. This, in turn, implied that Sky-Eyes had *grown up* in the company of his Spanish-speaking father. Had the man been a renegade, a deserter? Or, possibly, a man lost from his unit, unable to rejoin them? Díaz was encountering more and more questions, and few answers.

The Spanish of Sky-Eyes was spoken with an accent, he had noticed. The accent was vaguely familiar, he thought, but he could not place it. Ridiculous, he told himself. How could anyone tell what sort of accent might ensue from the use of Spanish by the Elk-dog People, whoever *they* might be.

The story of the strangers seemed plausible enough. They had furs to trade, though in only sample quantities. It was logical to come and see whether trade was practical before bringing an entire pack train. Díaz was inclined to believe the entire story. Simply natives from the plains, attempting to trade for much-needed steel knives and weapons, lance points and arrows for hunting. The pelt which they had presented him was of excellent quality, and should trade well.

Initially Spain had sought gold. Now, it appeared that the bounty of New Spain might include such things as furs and soft buffalo robes as well. Perhaps here was a new source of wealth.

"Shall we camp for the night, lieutenant?"

Sergeant Villa interrupted his thoughts.

"What? Oh yes, Sergeant. Let us make camp."

Sometime later, Díaz lay in his blankets, still puzzling over the strange encounter on the trail. He felt a great deal of responsibility over this. If the would-be traders were legitimate, it could be very good to have been the first to contact them. Surely, he thought, staring into the dying fire, surely they are as they seem. No one would take a woman on a mission that might be hazardous.

And what a woman, he reminded himself again. No, no one would bring such a wife on a mission with subterfuge involved. Unless . . . unless, he thought, this is a spy mission of some sort. No, surely not. Still . . . they pretend to be traders, but have little to trade. Their leader speaks Spanish fluently but with an accent. A woman . . . what better way to avoid suspicion than to bring a woman?

No, he told himself again. It is as Sky-Eyes says. He is a half-breed who considers himself of the Elk-dog People. They need knives and arrow points. Well, he had done the right thing to send the travelers to Captain Martínez. That relieved him of the responsibility.

Still, there was something that eluded him, something that his memory had noted, but that he now could not recall. Some incongruity, like the accent, which seemed so familiar, yet one he could not place.

He dozed, reliving for a moment the explanation of Sky-Eyes, about trading for knives and weapons for the hunt. The half-breed had started to clarify his mission by pointing to the knife at his waist, but had stopped before doing so.

Now, at the hypnotic stage of falling asleep, memory returned. The blue-eyed man had worn a knife, but had not taken it from its sheath as he talked. Díaz had noted the hilt, projecting from the decorated scabbard, and its shape had been vaguely familiar. Familiar, yet not really so. It was like the accent seen and heard before, but not the usual. Now, where had he seen such a knife hilt before? A more slender pattern than that of the Spanish hilt, but . . .

Suddenly, he sat bolt upright in his blankets.

"By Christ's blood!" he muttered to himself. *"French!"*

20

» » »

Díaz pulled on his boots and jumped to his feet. Purposefully, he strode toward the rumpled form that represented the sleeping sergeant.

Before he reached the blanket roll, however, he stopped short. No, he thought, perhaps it would be better not to rouse the troop. There was no way that they could overtake the presumed traders before they reached Santa Fe. A forced march would accomplish nothing, except the loss of a night's sleep and the exhaustion of the men and, more importantly, their horses.

He turned aside and threaded his way through the little camp toward the hillside. He needed to think this out. A sentry came to attention, and Díaz spoke to him as he passed. There was a jumble of boulders perhaps fifty paces outside the camp area, and it was here that the lieutenant chose to go. He sat on a convenient stone and took a deep breath of the crisp mountain air. Mother of God, what had he encountered?

The night was still, the stars seeming close enough to touch in their black velvet sky. To the east, a three-quarter moon was pushing its point above the horizon like a tongue of flame. He watched it for a moment, actually able to see it grow as it rose to break free of the darkness. A chorus of coyotes greeted its arrival, sending a shiver up the young lieutenant's spine. It was uncanny, how such a night, such a combination of natural sights and sounds could conjure up thoughts of the supernatural.

He shook his head to bring his thoughts back to reality. How was he to deal with his discovery? For that matter, he asked himself, what *was* his discovery? He had encountered a party of natives from an unknown tribe to the east, who claimed to be traders. He should have been suspicious when he saw that they had very little to trade. An excellent ploy, a means of entering Spanish territory for the purpose of spying.

The furs and robes that the intruders carried were, to be sure, of excellent quality. The pelt they had given him was of the finest. But would he not do the same, if he were placed in charge of a spy mission? Their explanation was plausible, of course. They had lost a horse, they had explained, when a cougar had frightened the animals. It was a possible thing, though somewhat unusual.

The makeup of the party was odd. Young warriors, except for the woman and the blue-eyed man who presented himself as her husband. Again he wondered, why would anyone bring a woman on a questionable venture such as this? Unless, of course, to diminish suspicion.

The other members of the party he had largely ignored. The sergeant had called his attention later to an odd fact. Two of the young warriors had worn buckskin shirts of a slightly different pattern. Their hair was also plaited in a different manner than that of the others. It seemed, Sergeant Villa had suggested, that these men might be of another tribe.

But of what significance was that, if any at all? He had talked a little further with the sergeant, who suggested that these two seemed to belong to a tribe that had traded in Santa Fe before on occasion. The others were of a new and different tribe. The man who called himself Sky-Eyes had appeared clean-shaven, or clean-plucked, as was the custom of some native tribes, the sergeant had said.

Díaz had brushed the information aside at the time. All natives looked alike, to some extent, though even he saw the different body and facial type in these prairie people. But now, the realization of the French possibility kept coming back to nag at him.

He tried to recall what he had heard before he left civilization, about the French and English. Those two countries were in heated confrontation over the northeastern portion of the New World. They were engaged in a drawn-out frontier war over domination of territory, the French to the north of the English. Both were pushing westward. But, Mother of God, had they pushed *this* far?

Spain had occupied the southern climes of the new continent. Except for a couple of probing expeditions into the plains, they had not attempted any exploration farther north than this. There was no wealth there anyway, as Coronado had clearly shown.

Now, here in northern New Spain, evidence of French contact had emerged unexpectedly. Well, so be it. There had been Spanish contact in the plains, too. The question was whether this was of any significance. He tried to reconstruct a scenario that would explain this strange turn of events.

Could there be a French outpost with native tribes as allies, sending a cleverly assembled party to spy out information? The blue-eyed man was obviously highly intelligent, multilingual, and a leader, of sorts. The sort of man who would be trusted with such an expedition.

What information did they seek? Were the French considering a move into New Spain, with this innocuous-looking party as the first information-gathering force?

Díaz was greatly troubled. Perhaps he should have ordered the strangers killed. But no, that would serve no purpose. If the French had designs on New Spain, they would only send more spies. No, it was better that the strangers be left alive, at least until they could be questioned. Dead, they could give no answers. Alive, and in Santa Fe, they could be watched, questioned, perhaps even tricked into revealing their identity and purpose.

Yes, he had done well, Díaz told himself, to send them to Captain Martínez. He had great faith in the captain's wisdom. Perhaps the two of them could plan how to deal with the situation. Perhaps it need go no higher in the chain of command. If they exposed a plot, he and Martínez would reap great prestige and possible promotion.

On the other hand, the story of the strangers *could* be true. Though it seemed unlikely, if things turned out that way, the two officers might benefit financially from the advance knowledge of coming trade.

Yes, Díaz finally convinced himself, he had handled the problem well. The suspects would be in Santa Fe when he arrived back from patrol. There was no way for them to escape, nowhere to go.

Martínez would have had an opportunity to form an opinion, and they could compare their impressions. Then they could plan a course of action, even before consulting higher-ups in the command. They should be able to use this situation to advantage, no matter what the outcome.

Personally, Díaz rather hoped that the story of the traders was true. Why not? A French half-breed, living with his mother's people, trying to establish a trade contact with civilization. Such a man would know nothing of international politics.

Then how, the haunting thought came back at him, how did Sky-Eyes have such a fluent command of Spanish? Doubts returned, and Díaz became depressed again. He had rather liked the blue-eyed leader of the traders. He hoped it would not be necessary to kill him.

21

» » »

In retrospect, Sky-Eyes thought that the initial encounter with the Spanish had gone rather well. He had managed to pass himself to the soldiers as a half-breed living with his mother's people.

At least, he thought so. One could never be quite certain. The lieutenant, Díaz, appeared intelligent, though young and inexperienced. His quickness, aided by the old sergeant's sage advice, would quickly make him a good officer.

That must be the way of the military in any country, Sky-Eyes pondered. Inexperienced young officers often owed their future careers to the wisdom of some taciturn old soldier who would never rise above the rank of sergeant. He had evaluated the relationship of Lieutenant Díaz and the sergeant at his side as such a situation.

So, it followed, the success of their trading mission might easily depend on the wisdom and integrity of three men: Díaz, the sergeant, and their captain, whom the traders had yet to meet. Ah, well, there was nothing to do but travel on.

They entered the village of Santa Fe from the east, winding through a street lined with adobe structures. His companions were astonished by the number of dwellings. Sky-Eyes, too, would have been impressed, he realized, if he had never seen Quebec, Montreal, and the great cities of Europe. It was difficult for him to remember that, with all her travels and worldly experience, Pale Star had never seen a modern city. Fort Mishi-ghan, a frontier outpost, was as close as she had come to civilization. For the others, except Turkey Foot, this was completely new.

They passed an adobe church or mission, with its cross at the top.

"Sky-Eyes, that is the sign of the medicine man at Fort Mishi-ghan," she observed, pointing to the cross. "Why is this so? Are they the same?"

He was at a loss for a moment. How could he explain the fact that in the civilized world, enemies could worship the same god? They could actually, he now realized for the first time, call on the same god to assist in the destruction of each other. He feared that any explanation would be ineffective.

It was a humbling experience, this look at the religion of his childhood through the eyes of the People. He remembered the occasion of his first notice of Pale Star. A priest back in Mishi-ghan had been lecturing a group of natives, telling the creation story. When Star had attempted to join in the storytelling, as was the native custom, she had been rebuked by the priest, lectured soundly, and accused of blasphemy. The courage and dignity of the girl had attracted Sky-Eyes' attention as she accused the priest of intolerance.

Aiee, that seemed long ago. It was before they had even met, long before they had become lovers.

"Star," he began tentatively, "you remember the creation story of my people?"

"About First Man and First Woman, and the real-snake?"

"Yes. These people have the same one."

"*Aiee!* The same beginning-story? But they speak different tongues!"

"Yes. But they have the same Great Spirit."

"That is why they use this sign?"

She crossed her forefingers to indicate the cross.

"Yes. That sign is used by the people of many tongues."

"They call their Great Spirit by the same name?"

"Yes. Well, it may be different in different tongues."

"Of course. But tell me, Sky-Eyes, it is all the same Great Spirit?"

"I suppose so."

He was a little uneasy over this discussion. What was she driving at?

"Then their Great Spirit, and ours, and the Growers', and the Head Splitters', all the same by different names, no?"

"Well, I . . ."

"It is good, Sky-Eyes. Looks Far once told me about this. When he and Wolf's Head made medicine together long ago, they decided. There are many paths to the top of the mountain, but they all lead to the top of the mountain."

She relaxed as they rode on, her questions apparently answered. Once more, Sky-Eyes felt humbled by the clear-thinking simplicity of the People's philosophy. And, of course, by Pale Star's grasp of it. He had first been smitten by her beauty, then by her intellect, then by both. Who else had he ever known who could sum up the entire meaning of theology in a sentence or two?

"Yes, it is good," he agreed.

They now entered an open rectangular area nearly a bow shot in length.

"The plaza," Turkey Foot pointed. "Their chiefs live in that big lodge."

The "big lodge" was truly imposing. It was the largest adobe structure that Sky-Eyes had ever seen. Even the size of the logs used in the construction of door and window openings was impressive. The ends of the massive beams that formed the flat roof projected out over a promenade or walkway along the building's front.

Uniformed sentries paced along the promenade, and one was stationed at the largest doorway. A Spanish flag fluttered from a staff in front. This appeared to be a headquarters building of some sort. Perhaps even the seat of the territorial government, he wondered.

"Turkey Foot, do you know anyone we can contact?"

"No. When I was here, others did that. Should we pay a visit to their chief?"

That would be logical protocol in their plains country, and might have merit here. However, Sky-Eyes doubted that the governor of the territory would give audience to a small party of native traders.

"I think not, Turkey Foot. We will look for the chief Martínez that the other young chief told us of."

They halted near the center of the plaza and dismounted to look around. The large building dominated most of one side of the square, and on the other sides were a polyglot assortment of shops and other buildings which appeared to dispense everything from food, drink, and lodging to live poultry. Long strings of the ever-present red chiles dangled from overhanging roofed walkways, with strings of onions and varicolored corn.

"Wait here," suggested Sky-Eyes, "I will ask about the Martínez-chief."

He strolled over to the promenade, a little stiff from the saddle, and approached a pacing sentry.

"Good day," he began, in the soldier's own tongue. "I seek for Captain Martínez."

The man stared arrogantly.

"And who are you?"

"I am called Sky-Eyes, of the Elk-dog People. The lieutenant, Díaz, told me to ask for Captain Martínez."

The sentry relaxed his uncompromising arrogance just a trifle. Sky-Eyes could see that the man was a bit more cautious. After all, if this traveler knew some of the garrison's officers by name, it would be well not to offend him. At least, until more information was forthcoming. Sky-Eyes smiled to himself at the transparency of the man.

"Come, tell me," he asked again, showing a bit more authority in his tone, "where I can find Captain Martínez!"

"Oh. Yes, I will take you there," answered the puzzled soldier. "Follow me."

He led the way down the promenade to a doorway in the building's outside wall.

"In there," he pointed awkwardly.

The sentry turned and resumed his pacing, wondering, no doubt, why he had shown such respect to a half-breed traveler from the country.

22

» » »

Sky-Eyes stepped through the open doorway into the cool of the building. It required a few moments for his eyes to become adjusted to the dusky interior after the brilliance of the afternoon sun. He was standing in a hallway perhaps two long paces wide, which led on into the structure. To his left ahead was a doorway, closed by a heavy plank door bound with rough-forged iron straps and rivets.

Across the hall, dim light shone through an open doorway. He stepped forward and looked into the room. It was a small anteroom, opening into the captain's office beyond. A uniformed clerk sat at the desk in the anteroom, scribbling with a quill pen on a sheet of paper. He had seen a hundred rooms like this, complete with the corporal at the desk. The only difference was the uniform of the orderly, which was not French, but Spanish.

The man looked up.

"Excuse me, sir," Sky-Eyes began, "I seek Captain Martínez."

The orderly looked him up and down, a little disdainfully, perhaps.

"And who are you?" he demanded.

"I am called Sky-Eyes. I have come far to see the captain."

He was becoming irritated by the manner of these soldiers. The clerk looked him over at length, and finally pointed to a wooden bench against the wall.

"Sit there," he said flatly.

Sky-Eyes sat. The corporal watched him for a few moments, and then returned to his report.

Sky-Eyes waited, listening to the scratch of the quill pen, and becoming more and more impatient. He was certain that the captain was in his office. He could hear the small sounds that a person makes, merely by breathing, swallowing, and moving around in a chair. He knew exactly what was going on. The captain was in, was not occupied, and the orderly was making him wait merely to demonstrate his own importance.

Sky-Eyes fumed. He would not have tolerated such insolence in his capacity as a French officer. But again he had to remind himself, he was no longer in such a capacity. He was merely a half-breed trader. At least, so these people would regard him.

His frustration grew. He considered pushing past the corporal, or demanding to be admitted at once. Both possibilities were rejected. Either would be self-defeating, and quite possibly dangerous. Instead, he sat quietly and watched a tiny ray of sunlight creep slowly across the floor, and listened to the scritch-scratch of the clerk's pen.

"Damn!" the corporal suddenly exclaimed.

His quill had snagged its tip on the surface of the page instead of gliding smoothly, spattering ink across the report. The corporal sat staring at the mess, still swearing under his breath. He rummaged around the desk-top, searching for blotting sand to sift onto the drying ink. Sky-Eyes smiled to himself, partly out of sympathy. The clerk's report would need to be redone, in all likelihood. The man sifted fine sand from a pewter box onto the page, and shook it gently dry before returning the blotting material to its container. Then he held the sheet up to the light, still cursing to himself. He seemed to notice the waiting Sky-Eyes.

"Are you still here?" he exploded. "Go on in!"

Sky-Eyes refrained from any of the remarks that came to mind. He stepped around the desk and entered the inner office. Again, he thought, this could be any one of a hundred offices he had seen before, except for the obvious. The tricolor flag which hung limply from its staff behind the desk was that of Spain, not France. The uniform of the captain, likewise.

"Captain, your Lieutenant Díaz sent me to speak with you."

The officer looked up from the papers on his desk, and seemed startled to see that his visitor wore the skin garments of a native. He studied Sky-Eyes for a moment, a question in his face.

"You know Lieutenant Díaz?" he asked cautiously.

"Not really, sir. We encountered his patrol on the trail yesterday."

"What trail? Who are you?"

"From the east, sir. I am called Sky-Eyes, of the Elk-dog People."

"I do not know the Elk-dog People. What is your purpose here?"

"We wish to trade. We have skins such as this."

Sky-Eyes drew out a selected pelt and presented it to the captain. He was beginning to worry a little about how many palms they must grease before they could do business. After all, their resources were limited. Ah, well, he decided, we can afford to give the whole load away this time, if we are successful in setting up another trip. If not, he reminded himself, they would be in trouble and it would not matter anyway.

Martínez stroked the soft fur and seemed to study the situation, without answering. Sky-Eyes' glance roved around the room, taking in the heavy furniture, the sword in its scabbard hanging from a peg behind the captain's desk. To the officer's left was a large map, of military style. Sky-Eyes immediately spotted Santa Fe near the center of the map, and the meandering trail to the mountain pass in the northeast, marked Raton.

"What do you want?" Martínez said curtly.

There was something about his tone that smacked of suspicion, and assured that he disapproved of the visitor's interest in the military map.

Sky-Eyes spread his hands placatingly.

"Only to trade, sir. We would trade furs and robes for

knives, iron to make arrowheads and spear points. It is as I told Lieutenant Díaz."

"Why do you come to me?"

"The lieutenant suggested it, sir. We know no one here."

"I see. Do you have many skins like this?"

"Only a few on this trip. If we can trade, we will return with a pack train next season."

Martínez was silent a little longer, apparently still suspicious.

"How is it that you speak Spanish?" he asked suddenly.

This time Sky-Eyes was more prepared for such a line of questioning.

"I learned it as a child," he said easily. "My father was a hairface."

"Yes, I wondered about your eyes. They give you a name, however," he chuckled. "Are there many Spanish in your country?"

"No, sir. None at all, now. I am a man of the Elk-dog People."

Sky-Eyes said the last with a great show of pride and bravado, hoping to establish not only those characteristics, but to distract the captain from his line of thought.

"Yes, of course," Martínez agreed. "You are with your mother's people."

The captain had accepted this status with little difficulty. Well, Sky-Eyes reflected, he must look the part. His dress, his hair, footwear, all pointed to his tribal status. His skin was burned brown by the sun and wind of the prairie. Except for the eyes, he could be easily taken for a native, he thought with some degree of pride.

"Where is the rest of your party?" Martínez asked.

"Outside."

"Well, it grows late. Find a place to camp, and come back in the morning. Then we will help you find some traders."

"Thank you, sir. I will return."

He turned from the room, resisting the impulse to salute as he was dismissed. The corporal at the desk was attempting to remove the ink blots from his report by careful scraping with a pen knife. Might as well go ahead and recopy it, Sky-Eyes said to himself.

"Thank you, Sergeant," he said aloud.

A little flattery never did any harm. He might need this man's help in some way. He was still not certain whether to trust Díaz and Martínez. Well, they could discuss it over the camp fire tonight. Most things were better discussed over a council fire, anyway.

The shadows were beginning to lengthen as he stepped outside, but the sun's rays in his face made him stop to blink a moment before orienting himself to the plaza. He started forward a step or two, scarcely glancing at the pacing sentry, and then stopped short.

The plaza was empty, except for a couple of sleepy-looking natives lounging under a tree. His companions, the horses and packs had vanished, as if none of it had ever existed.

23

» » »

Sky-Eyes whirled and trotted over to the pacing sentry. The man stopped and brought his short lance to a readier position.

"Where are my friends?" Sky-Eyes demanded.

"What are you talking about?"

"The rest of my party. Four men, a woman, horses, a pack horse."

"I saw no one. Move along!"

Sky-Eyes, on the verge of reaching for his belt-ax, paused a moment. He must be very cautious, now, keep his wits about him. He studied the sentry. Yes, this was a different soldier. The sentries had changed shifts while he had been inside.

"There was no one in the plaza when you came on watch?" he asked politely.

"Just the usual. No one like you."

The sentry looked Sky-Eyes up and down as if to emphasize his differences.

"Look," Sky-Eyes persisted, "I must see Captain Martínez again."

The sentry apparently decided it must be all right. After all, this strange-looking outsider had just come from the captain's office.

"All right," he grumbled. "Go ahead."

Sky-Eyes almost ran back into the building, and brushed past the frustrated corporal.

"Captain," he demanded, "my party is gone! Do you know anything of this?"

Martínez half rose from his desk in anger. He was obviously not accustomed to such insolence. Sky-Eyes struggled to check his emotions.

"I am sorry, sir, but my friends, horses, all our goods, are gone, while I was in your office!"

The captain sat back in his chair and spread his hands in a gesture of perplexity.

"How could I know this?" he asked. "I have been here!"

Sky-Eyes paused. Of course. He had acted like an idiot. He had imagined that they had been arrested and imprisoned, or worse. It seemed apparent that Captain Martínez could know nothing about this disappearance, since he had been with Sky-Eyes at the time.

"Captain, please tell me of the procedure here," he persisted. "Would such a party be arrested or detained?"

"Of course not. Unless, of course, their motives were in question."

"Their motives?"

"Yes, if they acted suspiciously, or were known to intend harm."

"But these people . . . my God, Captain . . . look, what is the chain of command? Could someone else have ordered them arrested?"

He saw again for a moment the look of displeasure that had darkened the face of the captain when he had noticed Sky-Eyes' interest in the map.

"I think not," Martínez said coldly.

Yes, it would be well to avoid questions about the command.

"Captain, I am a stranger here. Are there those who might wish us harm?"

Sky-Eyes was almost pleading, and the expression on the captain's face seemed to soften.

"Possibly. There are elements who prey on the unsuspecting. I will try to help you. Look, what are your arrangements for a place to stay?"

"None. We will camp outside of town for the night. We would decide when I rejoined them."

"Could they have gone to make camp?"

"We had not decided on a place."

"Yes. Well, let me inquire. You go ahead and look for them, and I will notify the patrols to be on watch for them. Come back in the morning."

It seemed little enough to do in assistance, Sky-Eyes told himself, but after all, what else could the captain do? He had offered to inquire. Beyond that, there was little that he could do. From Martínez' viewpoint, this was not an emergency. He undoubtedly had much greater worries each day in the administration of his job.

If, of course, the captain was telling the truth. He seemed cooperative and straightforward, but there was always a doubt. It could even be routine protocol to arrest strangers and impound their goods. Well, there was no more to be accomplished here.

"Thank you, Captain," he said politely. "I will return in the morning."

Martínez watched him go, and rose to follow him to the door. The man who called himself Sky-Eyes strode purposefully across the plaza. Even in his buckskin shirt, Martínez thought as he watched, there was something military about the stranger. His long stride was more like the marching step of a soldier than the easygoing saunter of a native.

There were other strange things about the man. He had shown great interest in the map, and in the command of the garrison at Santa Fe. These were not the interests of a half-breed from the prairie.

The whole demeanor of the man was puzzling. He had stood in the office and carried on a conversation as an equal. Then when he returned in anger, he had been quite demanding. Martínez had feared for a moment there that he would have to order the man arrested.

And what had happened to the fellow's party? It would be most unfortunate if they were completely on the level, and had fallen victims to one of the shadowy bands of highwaymen that frequented the area occasionally. No, surely not right in the plaza in front of the Governor's offices.

One more mystery remained, however. Lieutenant Díaz had encountered these people, and had directed them to him. The captain had a great deal of respect for the judgment of young Díaz. Had the lieutenant spotted something about these travelers that was not obvious to casual observation? Was there something that he, Martínez, had missed?

Probably nothing of overwhelming importance, he decided. If there were, Díaz would have cut short his patrol and returned to report it. But his patrol was still out. It must be that whatever had caused Díaz to direct the travelers to his office, it was important but not of an emergency nature.

Well, it seemed that there was nothing now but to wait. The captain hoped that the man Sky-Eyes would find his party. That would answer some annoying questions. Even more, he hoped that Díaz would hurry back from his patrol. There was possibly something known to Díaz that would help in his evaluation. But, the patrol might not return for another day, maybe two, unless their information was important.

Martínez sauntered back to his desk, and sat down. It was very frustrating, this confining duty. He would rather be out on patrol, riding the mountain trails on a good horse and breathing clean air. He had welcomed advancement, but now envied young Díaz.

"Captain," the orderly called from the outer office, "Lieutenant Díaz is coming in with his patrol. I thought he was not due back until tomorrow."

24
» » »

Pale Star and the others had waited uneasily after Sky-Eyes disappeared into the big lodge. The afternoon dragged along and nothing happened. Though these were people who were patient by nature, they were in unfamiliar surroundings, and suspicious of the unknown.

They had dismounted, and squatted at ease in the plaza, resting after the long ride. The pack horse stamped impatiently.

"Should we loosen his load?" asked Lean Bear.

"No, we would have to repack," Star assured him. "Sky-Eyes will return soon."

But Sky-Eyes still did not return.

"Should someone go and see what is happening?" wondered Turkey Foot.

Lean Bear smiled.

"I think if there is trouble, we would hear of it."

Yes, that seemed likely. If there had been a commotion of any sort in the Big Lodge, surely they would have heard some hint of excitement. Sky-Eyes, if he had encountered trouble, would have at least shouted to warn them. And the pacing sentry had shown no hint of any departure from the sleepy, dull routine of the day.

"Sky-Eyes will be all right," Pale Star announced, perhaps a little more confidently than she actually felt.

Over at one side of the square, three men lounged casually. They had been there when the travelers entered, watching curiously. After some time, they rose and saun-tered over to where the horses stood. They were talking among themselves, chuckling and pointing to the packs and the animals. Lean Bear moved nearer the pack horse.

The three strangers, dirty and nondescript, became bolder and more talkative. The leering gaze of the fat one who seemed to be their leader now focused on Pale Star. He pointed to the woman and made an apparently obscene re-mark, as the others chuckled and leered. Turkey Foot shifted over to stand beside her.

"It is all right, I will handle it," Star told him softly.

She shifted her belt-ax to a more prominent position at her waist. The three men laughed, but retreated. One made an obscene gesture.

They turned their attention again to the horses, circling and talking to each other in exaggerated tones. The travelers were at a disadvantage, unable to understand one word of the jocular conversation.

The intruders became bolder. The fat one stood looking at the pack horse, pointing to the bundled furs. Still talking, he cast a sidelong glance at the travelers, scratching the fringe of unkempt beard along his jaw.

That one, Star said to herself. That one is the dangerous one. Fat and physically out of condition though he might be, he would be the instigator of any trouble, because he would goad the others on.

The fat one now walked boldly over to the pack horse and began to feel a robe that was exposed at the corner of the bundle.

"Should I kill him?" asked Lean Bear, astonished at the man's lack of common courtesy.

"Not here," warned Turkey Foot, "in the middle of his own camp."

"But he must be stopped."

Lean Bear stepped forward, showing his bow with a read-ied arrow quite prominently. The fat one turned, eyes glit-tering, and a shiny medicine knife appeared in his hand. He appeared to realize that the travelers would not be so bold as to attack him in his own territory.

"Wait!" called Star. "We cannot fight here."

"Yes," agreed Turkey Foot, "if we have to fight, let it be in the open, not closed in by lodges on all sides."

They were all feeling the stress of being surrounded, threatened by the closeness of the unfamiliar adobe dwellings. It was a panicky feeling, a need to break through into the open country. There, they would feel confidence. The presence of the three men who were staring covetously at their packs of furs and at Pale Star was threatening, disconcerting. It was an unfamiliar situation, not one of fear, exactly, but of frustration.

"We need to get out of this camp," observed Turkey Foot.

The fat intruder was again toying with the fur packs. He seemed about to loosen the thongs that held the pack in place.

"Yes, we should leave," agreed Pale Star. "Sky-Eyes can find us. Remember, he spoke of the camping place that we saw this afternoon? He will look for us there."

The others nodded. They had passed a pleasant spot, where a clear stream circled a little meadow. Sky-Eyes had called attention to the place, almost within sight of Santa Fe, they now realized.

"A good place to camp," he had observed.

Now it seemed perfectly logical to assume that Sky-Eyes would know that was where they would go. He would look for them there.

"Shall we leave his horse?" asked Lean Bear.

"No! These dung-eaters would steal it!" retorted Star. "Let us make camp, and then someone can bring a horse and come back to get him."

In the urgency of the moment, this course of action seemed reasonable. Just now, it was imperative to break free of the threatening strangers who were becoming bolder. Lean Bear swung to the saddle and kneed his horse forward to take the lead rope of the pack horse. For a moment, it appeared that the fat leader of the intruders might block his way. Bear let his hand drop to the handle of the war club at his waist. It was a heavy, ugly weapon, indicating why his tribe were called "Head Splitters." The would-be thief smiled ingratiatingly and backed away, talking rapidly in his own tongue. Lean Bear reached to take the rope and started across the plaza, leading the pack horse.

Pale Star was leading the horse of Sky-Eyes, the rest of the party straggling after. The three men who had been harassing them barely stepped aside to let the horses pass, laughing and making gestures as if to seize the packs or equipment of the travelers. It was very tempting to settle the matter right there in the plaza.

Once, Crow reined in and reached for his war ax, but Star called out to him.

"Not here, Crow! If they follow us, maybe later."

It would not do to initiate a first contact with the town in a way to bring unfavorable attention.

They moved on, uneasy and on guard, retracing the route by which they had come. The three men followed alongside as far as the street, haranguing and laughing.

Just before they left the trio behind, the leader came alongside Star's horse for a moment, grinning through rotten teeth. She could smell the rank odor of the man as he brushed close to her horse and waved to catch her attention. He pointed to her and then to himself, talking and making gestures. She did not understand his tongue, but his crude sign-talk was unmistakable and highly suggestive.

Star sighed. She had encountered men like this before, in other times, places, and cultures. They would encounter this one again, and the result would likely be unpleasant. She rested a hand on her throwing ax and kneed the horse ahead.

25

» » »

Lieutenant Díaz rode up to dismount in the plaza, and was met by Captain Martínez. They exchanged perfunctory salutes.

"What is going on, Díaz?" the captain asked. "Who is this half-breed? Why have you returned?"

"Let us go inside, sir."

Díaz was unwilling to begin the conversation here on the promenade, before curious eyes and ears. The two men walked into the building and through the anteroom, Díaz brushing the dust of travel from his uniform. Martínez closed the door behind them.

"Captain, I do not know," Díaz began. "You have talked to the man who calls himself Sky-Eyes?"

"Yes, yes, go on," Martínez urged, meanwhile pouring a little brandy into a glass and handing it to the lieutenant.

"Thank you, sir. We have traveled hard."

"I know. And, you must have a reason."

"Yes, Captain, but I am not certain what it means. Did you notice the man's accent?"

"Of course. But he speaks Spanish well, for a native or half-breed."

"Exactly. He says he learned Spanish from his father, but how could that be? We have no outposts in the plains."

"No, but there have been some expeditions."

"But none to *stay*."

"Ah yes. I see your point. A renegade, perhaps?"

"I thought so at first, sir, but I noticed something else. Did you see his knife?"

"His knife?" Martínez asked, puzzled.

"Yes, his belt knife. It appeared to be of French pattern."

"French?"

"Yes, sir. Now, look at their party with that idea in mind."

"I did not see their party, only the one man. Did you arrest the others?"

Díaz' mouth dropped in astonishment.

"Arrest? Of course not. Why do you ask, Captain?"

Now Martínez was uneasy.

"When Sky-Eyes left my office, he rushed back in to report that his party was gone. Do you know what may have happened to them?"

"No, sir. It was my thought that we should not interfere with their movements until we know more of their intentions."

"My thoughts exactly. They cannot move far or fast. There is no place to go. That is why I did not detain them. But tell me, Díaz, of the rest of the party."

"Well, there are three or four men besides the leader, and one woman. She is the wife of the man, Sky-Eyes, or so they said. A beautiful woman, maybe thirty years old."

"Does she look like a native?"

"Yes, I think so. But, a real beauty."

"Does that strike you as odd, a woman on a trading expedition?"

"Maybe. I am puzzled, sir. In many ways, they seem exactly as they say. Natives of the plains, with furs to trade for iron knives and weapons. But, if their leader is French, perhaps a French officer . . ."

"Yes. There may be a French thrust into New Spain. This odd party has many traits of a spy mission."

"Should I arrest them now for questioning, Captain?"

Martínez spread his palms, perplexed.

"How? We do not know where they went. Except for Sky-Eyes, of course. He left just before your return."

"Yes, sir. Suppose I send men to find the others, without

disturbing them. At the same time, perhaps we can arrest Sky-Eyes before they join forces. You say he is on foot?"

"Yes. Excellent, Díaz. He has not had time to travel very far. Have him picked up and bring him here. Then watch the others."

"Captain," the lieutenant began uncertainly, "suppose it is as they say, and they wish only to trade furs."

He pointed to the soft pelt on the captain's desk.

"Then no harm is done. We help them. But now, go, Díaz, before we lose him. He took the east road."

Lieutenant Díaz turned and almost ran from the building, barking orders to his troopers as they mounted. Sergeant Villa, somewhat puzzled, took a few men to search for the camp of the strangers. The rest of the platoon followed the lieutenant at a quick trot.

Díaz did not know what to expect when (and if) they overtook the mysterious Sky-Eyes. Would the man immediately betray his true purpose? Not likely, he decided. If Sky-Eyes was actually a French spy, he would be shrewd enough not to jeopardize his mission as well as his life by admitting it. He would likewise probably not resist arrest, as that would be an admission of guilt.

The lieutenant sighed and realized that he was setting up a no-win scenario. For if the man resisted, it could also imply innocence, while apparent cooperation might mean that he was a spy.

There was no further time to think. They were nearing the outskirts of town, and in the fading light of day, he could see a tall figure in buckskins striding along the street.

"Remember, he is not to be injured," he admonished as he spurred forward, followed by the troopers.

Then from beyond the walking figure, a horseman approached, leading a riderless horse. Díaz recognized one of the other warriors. They arrived at the point where Sky-Eyes stood, almost at the same time. There was a moment of confusion as the horsemen milled uncertainly. The blue-eyed man stood quietly, his back against the adobe wall of the house behind him. The other warrior was trying to hand him the rein of the led horse, and Sky-Eyes seemed reluctant to take it. Díaz realized that to try to mount the horse while encircled by lancers would seem unwise, and that Sky-Eyes realized it. The man was no fool.

"Señor Sky-Eyes," he called.

"Yes, Lieutenant?"

The man's voice seemed calm and collected.

"Will you come with us?"

"It seems I have little choice. Am I under arrest?"

Díaz paused. He wished to be truthful.

"The captain wishes to talk with you again."

There, he had avoided the direct answer, at least for the present.

"What about Lean Bear, my companion?" Sky-Eyes asked.

"Let him tell your party where you are."

"May I have a moment to speak with him?"

"Of course. But only a moment. The captain waits. Where is your party?"

Sky-Eyes turned and questioned Lean Bear a moment.

"He says they are camped northeast of here, where there is water."

Díaz nodded.

"Tell them to wait there."

Sky-Eyes apparently relayed that information, and then turned back to Díaz.

"Must I walk?" he inquired.

"No, no, bring your horse."

Sky-Eyes now took the rein and swung to the horse's back. He spoke to Lean Bear in his own tongue, appearing to give instruction or information, and the warrior turned to trot slowly away. Sky-Eyes then turned his attention again to Díaz.

"Well, Lieutenant, shall we go?"

Díaz was uneasy. The demeanor of the man was too smooth, too polished. There was much that did not meet the eye. The entire situation had a feel that Díaz did not like. All the actions of this mysterious blue-eyed man fit exactly the actions of a spy.

26

» » »

The ride back to the plaza seemed endless. Díaz said nothing, merely rode in tight-lipped silence, so Sky-Eyes did not try to engage him in conversation.

As they rode, however, the thoughts of Sky-Eyes were racing. What had happened? Lieutenant Díaz had plainly indicated that his patrol was not due to return for another day or two. Why had he altered his assignment and returned early?

And Captain Martínez . . . they had seemed to get along in a rather congenial manner, it seemed. Then, after the return of Díaz and the patrol, the situation had suddenly changed. Here he was, under arrest. True, Díaz had not actually said so, but he had evaded the question. As a former lieutenant himself, Sky-Eyes certainly recognized an arrest. If a captain wishes merely to talk to someone, he does not send a mounted platoon of lancers to bring him in.

There had been a moment when Sky-Eyes had considered escape. He could duck between the buildings and lose himself in the gathering darkness. Then he saw Lean Bear approaching with an extra horse, and had a moment's urge to swing up and ride away. Common sense prevailed, however. Such a move would be quite stupid, with the lancers already near.

No, it was best to remain dignified and cooperative, at least until he learned more of the situation. Quickly, he had learned from Lean Bear that the others were safe, and that they had left the plaza simply to avoid the closed-in feel of a town. That was something of a relief, to know where they were camped. He could rejoin them when and if the captain chose to release him.

They were entering the plaza now, and Sky-Eyes saw that there were lights in some of the windows along the square. Díaz signaled a halt, and the troopers sat while the lieutenant dismounted.

"Come, señor," he invited. "Fernandez, take his horse."

Sky-Eyes stepped down, and reluctantly handed the rein to one of the troopers. A sentry saluted Díaz, and they walked into the building.

The anteroom was empty, but a candle burned on the desk. Díaz motioned for Sky-Eyes to precede him, and they moved through to the captain's inner office. It was brighter here, with a candle in a wall sconce, and two on the captain's desk. Martínez motioned the others to chairs, and sat back.

"Close the door, Díaz."

"Yes, sir."

The lieutenant complied, and then sat down. Martínez was studying the visitor, as if trying to make up his mind.

"Sky-Eyes," he spoke at last, "who in Christ's name are you?"

Sky-Eyes started to speak, but Martínez waved him to silence.

"There are many things about you that do not quite add up," he continued. "I know that you are not what you seem, but just what are you?"

The thoughts of Sky-Eyes were racing. What could he say? He had no desire to blurt out his entire history.

"Sir," he began cautiously, "what do you mean? Have I done something to offend the Captain?"

Martínez exhaled audibly.

"You tell me, señor."

"Captain, it is as I told you. What more can I say?"

"What more? You make this quite difficult, señor. Why is it, for instance, that only you, of all your party, speak Spanish?"

He hurried on, without waiting for an answer.

"How is it that your eyes, which give you your name, are blue? This would be unusual for a half-breed. Especially so if your father was Spanish. I do not believe that he was."

Sky-Eyes shrugged, hoping to appear nonchalant.

"Who knows, señor? To the People, one hairface looks much like another."

"But if you learned the tongue from him, you remember him well. Where was his home?"

"Far away across the Big Water, the sea. How would I know?"

Sky-Eyes realized that the situation was deteriorating rapidly. He wondered how much the captain had deduced. These two officers were surely perceptive.

"Señor Sky-Eyes," Martínez was saying calmly, "you will please to place your weapons on the desk, very slowly."

"Then I am under arrest?"

He looked around the room, at the closed door, at Díaz sitting like a coiled spring on the edge of his chair, hand on his sword hilt. Behind the captain, the weapon that had hung from the peg was no longer there. Sky-Eyes knew it must be behind the desk, hidden from view, but convenient to the captain's hand.

He took a long breath. He could make a break for it, but rejected the idea. He would never reach the door.

Slowly, he reached behind him and took his belt-ax from its place. He laid it carefully before him.

"The knife, too," Martínez urged.

The blade joined the ax on the captain's desk.

"Ah, as we thought. French!" Martínez announced triumphantly. "Where did you get this knife?"

"Señor, my people trade with many. There are knives, axes, pipe stone, arrow points from many places."

"Then if you have such things, why do you come here?"

Sky-Eyes felt trapped. He had, indeed, almost been tricked into what appeared to be a confession.

"For better trade, better quality of goods."

He knew that the explanation must sound fabricated.

"Sky-Eyes," the captain said coldly, "we think you are a French spy. Is your country pushing into New Spain?"

"Captain," Sky-Eyes pleaded, "if I were a French spy, would I carry that knife?"

The captain looked at Díaz, and both looked startled for a moment.

"Perhaps not," admitted Martínez, "but there is much you are not telling us. We will talk again in the morning. It may be that a night in a cell will help loosen your tongue."

He turned to the lieutenant.

"Díaz, arrest the others. We will question them, too."

"Captain," spoke Sky-Eyes urgently, "remember that none of them speaks Spanish. They can tell you nothing."

"We will see. Perhaps they will recall some skills."

"Please, señor. If you try to arrest them, they will fight, because they will not understand. Blood will be shed. Let me go with the lieutenant to translate."

Martínez was quiet a moment.

"Maybe it would be better," he mused. "Yes, that is reasonable. Díaz, take him with you in the morning. But, in irons."

"Sir," the lieutenant protested, "if they see him in irons, might that not incite them to resist?"

"Perhaps. But, we could just kill them all, without trying to question them. Well, as you wish, Díaz. Just make certain you do not lose this one. I am going to bed."

He rose and left the room.

"We go, now," stated Díaz. "Move slowly, ahead of me."

Two troopers moved forward as they came into the hallway. These, Sky-Eyes assumed, would escort him to the cell the captain had mentioned.

His heart was very heavy.

27

» » »

The cell was damp, slightly chilly, and had a musty smell, like the indefinable odor in a place where mice build their nests. It was an animal smell, and Sky-Eyes was reminded of the lodges of the Growers. He stood there a moment after the heavy ironbound door banged shut, allowing his eyes to begin to accommodate to the room. It seemed that he had been suddenly plunged into darkness, like a plunge into cold water. The dark now closed around him, and he could feel, rather than see, the confines of the walls.

The tiny slivers of light from the guard's lantern, which had shone through cracks in the door now wavered and disappeared. A very faint light from outside filtered through a barred window high in the wall. He felt cautiously around the tiny room to determine that he was alone, and that the cell was empty except for a pile of straw in one corner, apparently to serve as a bed. Little rustling noises in the straw gave a hint that perhaps he was not *entirely* alone. He shuddered a little, and resolved not to trust his person to the rodent-infested bed-pile.

Actually, even had it not been for the mice or rats, he was loathe to use the straw. There was no way of knowing what insect guests might remain from the last occupant of the cell. Sky-Eyes paced irritably, unwilling to sit down on the dirt floor when he could not see its surface.

He looked longingly at the window and the small rectangle of starry sky outside. The opening was higher than his line of vision, and he pulled himself up by the iron bars to look outside. There was only the deserted street. He turned and leaned against the wall, frustrated and anxious. What was Star doing? Would she be worried about his predicament? Of course, he told himself irritably.

He was glad that he had been able to speak for a moment with Lean Bear. At least, he now knew where the little band of would-be traders was camped. He would be able to see them in the morning.

Beyond that, their future seemed in doubt. The entire idea of trading with the Spanish seemed completely idiotic, here in the darkness of a Spanish jail cell. They could have been at home, among the People, enjoying the fine weather and good hunting for which the Moon of Ripening was noted. Instead, even their lives were in jeopardy. At very least, their furs and supplies would be seized, and possibly their horses also. The possibilities seemed slim.

Other possible events intruded on his troubled thoughts. What if, after questioning, presumably with Sky-Eyes as interpreter, the captain decided to keep him as a prisoner and free the others? He could hardly bear the thought of losing Star. That would be worse than the imprisonment. His concern for the party as they attempted to make their way back to their own country would be intolerable.

He thought of openly telling all to the captain, confessing that he had originally been sent to explore, but had chosen to remain with the People. No, he decided, that would not do. The story was too improbable to be believed. Especially, he told himself with a wry smile, especially when told by one who was an admitted deserter. There seemed no way out of the dilemma.

Later, he wondered how he had ever gotten through that terrible night without losing his sanity. He believed that it had been because of his association with the philosophy of the People, doing what could be done and then waiting to see what might be done next.

Just now, he felt that he was not handling the situation well at all. He wanted to scream out in frustration, to beat on the iron bars of the window. Instead, he paced the narrow cell, lifted himself to look out the window occasionally, and worried.

It seemed an eternity before the small square of starstudded black sky began to gray, and the intense darkness of the cell began to fade with a dim predawn light. Even longer before he heard the stirring of men awakening in other parts of the building. A rooster in the distance crowed to greet the rising sun. It was strange to hear so familiar a sound from his childhood in so far and remote a place.

Perhaps, he thought, at the proper moment his party could fight their way free. He quickly abandoned the possibility. It was too dangerous. Foolhardy, even, to think of attacking a superior force of professional soldiers. Even if some of them escaped, they were in country not their own, with few supplies. No, they could make no plans yet. They must wait to see which way the wind would blow.

Now he heard the approach of the jailer, the heavy jangle of keys, and the grate of the lock. It was still dark enough that the man carried a lantern. Behind him, Sky-Eyes saw the tall form of Lieutenant Díaz, who beckoned him forward. The lieutenant led the way to a room that appeared to be the office of the jailer. He pointed to a set of manacles on the table.

"Señor," he began, "I have been instructed to use those if I see fit. But, I understand your feeling that it might cause trouble."

"Yes, I think it might."

"I want no trouble. Only to get to the heart of this matter."

Sky-Eyes nodded, wondering where this conversation was headed.

"Now, I believe you know the meaning of gentleman's arrest. Am I correct?"

"Yes, señor."

There was nothing to be gained by denying such knowledge.

"Very well. We can avoid the irons if you pledge not to try to escape. Do I have your word?"

Sky-Eyes considered for a moment. What an odd situation! The Spanish lieutenant was prepared to accept his word as a military officer, even though no such relationship existed. Was this a trap? Would it appear, if he gave his promise not to escape, that this was proof of his military status? More specifically, proof that he was admitting that he was a French spy? It was all very complicated. He looked again at the manacles on the table, joined by a short length of chain. He had a dread of such things.

"You have my word, Lieutenant."

"Very well. Come."

They emerged into the open air just as the sun's rays reached across the area with the promise of a new day. Sky-Eyes drew in a deep breath of the crisp mountain air, thankful to be outside again.

The platoon of lancers stood ready to mount. A trooper led Sky-Eyes' horse forward, and he was pleased to see that the animal had been groomed, and probably fed. He smiled grimly. His captors had treated the horse better than he himself had been treated. Of course, in this country, it might be that a horse was worth more than the life of one man. It was a disconcerting thought.

Díaz gave the order, and the troopers swung to their saddles. Sky-Eyes vaulted to his own horse's back. For a moment, he resisted the temptation to stick heels into the animal's flanks and try to escape. It was only for a moment. He realized the futility of such an action, even if he had not given his parole.

The lieutenant gave the arm signal and the platoon moved forward. Sky-Eyes rode beside Díaz, with a pair of troopers ahead and the rest behind them.

For the hundredth time, Sky-Eyes wondered what this day might bring, and who might or might not be alive when Sun Boy crossed Earth's rim. Oddly, a phrase from the Death Song of the People flitted through his mind.

> The grass and the sky go on forever,
> But this is a good day to die.

28

» » »

Pale Star rose, shook out her sleeping-robe and rerolled it. It was not yet dawn, but she had slept very little anyway. Her concern over her husband would not allow it. They had been apart very little since discovering their mutual love after the tragic accident in the river. *Aiee*, that seemed a lifetime ago. She had pulled the unconscious Sky-Eyes from the hungry water that tried to claim his life. Now, he belonged to her. Or rather, they belonged together. It had taken only a little while for them to realize that.

Now, recent events had separated them. It was the first time, the very first night, that they had been apart by other than their own choice. She was worried about his welfare. True, Lean Bear had assured her that Sky-Eyes was all right, that he seemed healthy and unhurt. Lean Bear had seen the soldiers come and surround him, and Sky-Eyes had gone with them willingly, riding his own horse.

On one point Lean Bear was very definite. Sky-Eyes had insisted that they stay here and wait for him. They must not leave this camping place. Well, that was good enough. There was water, a little grass for the horses.

But Star was plagued with doubt. What if Sky-Eyes was in danger that he did not know? What if he was unable to return to them? The thought even occurred to her that it might be risky for him to see again the way of the Hairfaces. True, these were not of his tribe, but the suggestion was plain. When she first knew Sky-Eyes, he had been a lieuten-

ant, a young chief of the *Fran-coy*, much like the leader of
the soldiers they had met. She wondered if this contact with
the soldiers would make him miss his previous life. Would
he have regrets that he had abandoned his own tribe to become a man of the People?

Of course not, she told herself irritably. Sky-Eyes would
not be like that. Did he not, by all his ways, show her every
day that he had no regrets, that he preferred the lodge that
they shared to any spot on earth?

Star smiled to herself, reassured, but a fragment of gnaw-
ing doubt remained. She shivered in the chill of the morning and hugged her arms around her body. She walked up
the slope to where Crow squatted as a sentry.

"Go on, Crow," she greeted. "I will stand watch."

"Are you sure?" Crow asked softly.

"Yes. It is all right. I will not sleep anyway, and it is nearly
dawn."

The young man's sympathy was apparent.

"You wish me to stay with you?"

"No. I wish to think. But, thank you, Crow."

He drew his robe around him and strolled back toward the
camp. Star saw him begin to toss a few sticks on the coals of
last night's fire. It was time to rise and greet the day.

Star turned to look at the lightening sky along earth's rim
to the east. She wondered at what point Sun Boy would
thrust his torch. Probably by the jutting rock on that distant
hillside. Yes, she could see now, the spreading glow above
the distant mountains. A bright ray sparkled at the horizon,
blinding in its intensity, growing until she could no longer
look at its glory. Dawn had come, and in her heart she was
thankful for the new day. It was encouraging, uplifting in a
sense, the reassurance of Sun Boy's return, even here in a
strange country.

But what would this day bring? This thought made her
heart heavy. When Lean Bear had returned last night without Sky-Eyes, she had feared the worst. Bear did not seem
concerned, and brought a message from her husband. She
was forced to accept the situation, though unwillingly.
There was nothing she could do. In the chill of the mountain night, she had slept little, her sleeping robe cold and

lonely without the presence of Sky-Eyes. She recalled the dreadful nights on the riverbank, after the accident that brought them together. They had nothing, no supplies, and one thin blanket to share. They had been forced to snuggle together, to share body warmth for survival. That warmth had blossomed into love, and there had been few nights since that they had been apart.

Sun Boy's torch was nearly fully visible now, though, of course, no one could actually look at its grandeur. Star's companions were rising, yawning and stretching, walking a little way out of camp to urinate, and returning to the little routine chores of the morning camp.

She moved back to the fire, appreciating its warmth. Later, the day might be uncomfortably warm, but just now the heat was good. She stood with her back to the warmth, letting it drive the stiffness from her bones.

"Bear," she asked, "did Sky-Eyes say when he would return?"

"No," Lean Bear answered sympathetically. "Only that we wait here until he comes."

Star nodded. But how *long* should they wait? One day? Three? A moon? What if he did not return at all? That was a possibility she must face. Every time they were apart for a little while, she feared for his safety.

The life of the People was dangerous. At any time, a husband might not return from a hunt. There was much risk in riding into the herds of buffalo. Her friend Pink Cloud, first wife of Woodchuck, had been killed by a wounded bull in a freak accident.

There was always the possibility of a skirmish with warriors from another tribe. The People had been at peace in recent years, but there was the occasional adventurous party from outside who posed a risk. It was not like the constant all-out wars with the Head Splitters recounted by the older people, before their truce and alliance. Fortunately, it was not like the indiscriminant scalp-hunting of the tribes she had known in the Big Lakes country, either. Yet, a man killed in a minor skirmish was just as dead.

There was risk. Any woman of the People knew, when her man left the lodge, that this time he might not return. It was a way of life. Yet somehow, this situation was different. She had confidence in Sky-Eyes' ability to take care of himself in the hunt or in battle. Here, she did not know. Star could not visualize what situation he might find himself in, and the unknown made her uneasy. She wished she could be with him. She knew that at some point she could no longer stand the suspense, and must return to the town to see what was happening. It was not yet apparent to her how long she could wait before she must go.

One other thing concerned her. When that time came, not one of their party could communicate with the Spanish, or with the local natives. Sign-talk was almost unknown here. Turkey Foot knew a few words of Spanish, but not enough. Star herself had begun to learn as they traveled, but realized that her skills would not even begin to be adequate. The only person who could actually communicate here was Sky-Eyes, and he was a prisoner.

She could try to go to him when she could stand it no longer, but what good would it do? She would be unable, even, to ask questions as to where Sky-Eyes might be found.

A movement caught her eye, and she focused attention on it. From the direction of the town came a procession of soldiers, riding slowly. There was no way to tell their purpose, but she did not see how it could be good.

"Are your weapons ready?" she called. "The soldiers come!"

29
» » »

Sky-Eyes saw the camp of his companions ahead, saw them move quickly and become attentive to the approaching patrol. He knew they would be readying weapons, preparing for whatever might come. At all costs, he must avoid a skirmish. Not only would that doom their expedition to failure, but it would cost lives. He had seen the skills of Pale Star, years ago in the lake country of Mishi-ghan. Her use of the throwing-ax had been well known at the fort. There would be soldiers killed, and then the other soldiers would hunt down the survivors. *Aiee*, why had he agreed to this trading expedition? Life had been so simple.

Just now, he must do something, and quickly.

"Lieutenant," he asked, "may I ride in first and explain to them?"

He could follow the lieutenant's line of thought. The others could arm the prisoner, of course, but it would do them little good. The troopers outnumbered the little party by nearly three to one. There was no place to run or hide where they could not be hunted down. What harm could it do to let the prisoner ride ahead a short way?

"What will you tell them?" Díaz asked.

"That the captain wishes to question them."

"They must give up their weapons," Díaz insisted.

"Begging the Lieutenant's pardon, that would not be wise. It is a thing of pride for them."

"But you surrendered yours."

"Yes."

Sky-Eyes felt trapped again. He could not explain his different attitude without revealing why he was different.

"Where will you question them?" he asked.

Díaz shrugged.

"It is up to the captain, I suppose."

"Señor," Sky-Eyes proposed, "I do not know if they will allow themselves to be placed in cells."

"They have no choice!" Díaz snapped indignantly.

"No, but they might choose to fight and die instead."

"Then you must tell them. They will be killed."

"Lieutenant, you must understand. Most of the People have never been inside a building. Even a house looks like a trap. They live in skin tents, in the open."

"Mother of God! Is it cold there in winter?"

"Yes, yes. I will tell you about it. But now, time grows short. May I ride ahead?"

Díaz hesitated only a moment.

"Yes, go on. But I will be watching."

He motioned the platoon to a halt, and Sky-Eyes kneed his horse forward. Díaz kept the troopers at a little distance. Pale Star ran to meet her husband.

"Sky-Eyes! Are you all right? They have not hurt you?"

"No, of course not."

He dismounted and gave her a quick hug.

"Come, listen, all of you," he called, motioning them to him. "We must go and pay our respects to the chief."

"To this young chief?" Turkey Foot inquired, pointing to Díaz.

"No, to his chief."

"Is this the usual custom, Sky-Eyes?" asked Star, somewhat suspicious.

"Sometimes," he answered honestly. "They wish to question us about why we come."

"Then you talk to them," Lean Bear suggested. "None of us speaks their tongue."

"Yes, I have done so. But they wish to talk to the rest."

"Sky-Eyes!" Star exclaimed suddenly. "Your weapons. Where are they?"

"I have left them in the big lodge where we were last night."

"Why?" insisted Star. Then realization seemed to dawn. "You are still a prisoner."

"Yes. I have given my promise not to escape."

"*Aiee!*" exclaimed Turkey Foot. "Bear said you went willingly! Look, I will hand you my lance. We will fight our way free!"

"No!" insisted Sky-Eyes sharply. "We would be killed."

"But what do they want, Sky-Eyes?" Star insisted, bewildered.

"They think I am a French spy," he told her.

The others seemed confused. It was not easy to explain the situation, but he must try.

"Listen," he explained, "my tribe and this one, the Spanish, both want to come into the plains. Their chief thinks I have come as a spy."

"Then tell them, Sky-Eyes!" insisted Lean Bear. "Tell them it is not true."

"I have told them, Bear. But they want to ask you."

Lean Bear shook his head.

"The ways of the Hairfaces are strange," he admitted.

Díaz appeared restless, and Sky-Eyes hurried on.

"Bring all our packs," he urged, "and let us go."

Star lingered by him for a moment.

"Sky-Eyes, are we to be prisoners?" she asked grimly.

"No, I think not. Not yet."

"We keep our weapons?"

"Yes. I have spoken of that with the young chief."

"This is not good, Sky-Eyes."

"I know. We can do nothing else."

"If the time comes, we can fight."

"And be killed?" he retorted.

"Maybe not," she said grimly.

The others were mounted now, and the soldiers parted to let them move down the trail, falling into double file ahead and behind.

Star's thoughts were fluttering rapidly ahead. This was not good. She felt that they were moving into a trap. Something must be done to convince the Spanish of their good

faith. Sky-Eyes had been unable to do so. Why? she pondered.

"Sky-Eyes, what did you tell them?" she asked as they
rode.

"What do you mean?"

"They asked if you are French?"

"Yes. I told them my father was a blue-eyed Hairface from
far away. That is true."

"Yes. You did not tell them that you were once French,
before you became a man of the People?"

"No."

Star rode for a little way, beginning to understand. Her
husband was a proud man. He would not demean himself by
admitting that he was a deserter. His loyalties had been too
strong. She well remembered the quarrel between Sky-Eyes
and Woodchuck. Each had accused the other of desertion,
and they had nearly come to blows.

Somehow, she must make the Spanish know that her husband was not a spy. If he would not explain to them, then
she must. But how? She knew only a few words of their
tongue. Any questioning, any explanation must be through
Sky-Eyes as interpreter, and he would not agree to translate
such an explanation. What could she do, with none of their
tongue and no sign-talk? If she could only talk with them, as
she had learned to do with the *Fran-coy* in Mishi-ghan. She
had picked up the French tongue fairly rapidly after her arrival. People in contact with other tongues often did so just
by repeated contact, she knew. Just as the People and the
Head Splitters used each other's tongues. Just as Sky-Eyes,
though the language of his tribe was French, had learned
Spanish.

She stopped short. Was that the answer to her dilemma? If
the French and Spanish were in contact in their own land,
then . . .

Very casually, she reined her horse over to visit with Lean
Bear for a little while, making small talk about the soldiers.
She did the same with Beaver Tooth and then rode alongside
Lieutenant Díaz for a few moments. When the time was
right, she spoke softly.

"Parlez-vous français?"

"Mother of God! You speak French?" Díaz exploded, in his own tongue.

"Shh," she warned.

She turned to look at her husband, but he was in conversation with Lean Bear.

"You speak French?" Díaz asked, more softly and now in that language.

Star was elated.

"Yes. I must speak to you or to your chief. I can answer your questions."

Díaz nodded.

"I can arrange it."

He spurred his horse and rode on, nonchalantly and without further comment.

30

» » »

Lieutenant Díaz led his little caravan into the plaza and dismounted. He turned to Sky-Eyes.

"Come with me."

"You will not try to take their weapons?"

"My troops will start no trouble unless yours do. Tell your people to wait here."

He gave a command and the lancers dismounted. Díaz pointed to two men and motioned them to follow, then led the way into the building, followed by Sky-Eyes and the two troopers. Once inside, he stopped.

"Señor," he spoke politely, "they will take you back to your cell."

"No!" insisted the prisoner. "None of them can speak to you. I am needed!"

"Señor Sky-Eyes," Díaz spoke firmly, "I would like to believe your story. I think you have spoken truth, though maybe not the entire truth. Please believe that I am trying to help you. I will send for you when you are needed. Now, please go."

Sky-Eyes stood for a moment, and seemed to realize that he had little choice. He nodded and walked on down the hallway, flanked by the troopers. Díaz stepped into the captain's office, nodded to the clerk, and moved on into the inner office. The captain looked up from his map-littered desk.

"Ah, Díaz, you have them in custody?"

"Yes, sir, in a manner of speaking. They are outside. There is something else we must speak of."

"Well, go on."

"The woman, Captain. She wishes to see us, alone."

Martínez chuckled.

"Why? She wants to sleep with us in return for her husband's release?"

Lieutenant Díaz reddened, somewhat irritated. He had not even considered such an interpretation.

"It is not like that, Captain. This woman is a lady."

"I thought she is a native."

"Yes, sir. But you have not met her. This is an unusual woman. She has offered to answer our questions. Oh, yes, she speaks French."

"*French?* Ah, we were right!"

Martínez rubbed his palms together.

"Possibly, sir. But I think you should talk with her. I have sent her husband back to the cell to separate them."

"Good. Very well, Díaz, bring her in."

Díaz left the office, but quickly returned, accompanied by Pale Star. Martínez, obviously prepared to be unimpressed and immovable, was caught completely off guard.

The appearance of this woman was so striking that an observer was forced to take notice. She was tall, with a well-turned body and fine features. Her large, wideset eyes were dark and intense, with a penetrating depth that was striking to observe. Above all was her demeanor. The woman carried herself with such poise, dignity, and confidence that an observer was struck with the impression of royalty. Even in her buckskins, her appearance seemed to demand respect. Captain Martínez, confused, found himself rising to his feet to honor his visitor and offer her a chair.

He moved back around the desk to his own seat, trying to regain his composure. Very formally, he began with words of greeting in French.

"Good morning, *madame*. Lieutenant Díaz tells me you are fluent in the use of French."

The woman smiled.

"Not fluent, perhaps, Captain. Enough to talk. How may I help you?"

Martínez was caught off guard again. He had expected almost anything but this approach. Begging, pleading perhaps. Here was a woman who calmly asked with pride and dignity how *she* might help. The captain looked around the room and noticed Díaz still standing near the doorway, an amused smile on his face.

"Sit down, Lieutenant. Close the door first."

He turned again to the woman seated across from him.

"*Madame*, will you answer some questions for us?"

"Of course, Captain, if I am able."

Her entire attitude radiated quiet confidence and cooperation. Martinez was still ill at ease. Lieutenant Díaz was enjoying this encounter immensely.

"Very well," the captain began. "Suppose you tell us of yourself. Who are you?"

"I am called Pale Star. My nation is the People. We are sometimes called the Elk-dog People because we used horses earlier than some."

"And your country is the plain?"

"Yes, Captain."

"How far?"

"About a moon's travel."

"This man, Sky-Eyes, your leader. He is your husband?"

"Yes. My husband. He is our leader on this journey because only he can speak your tongue."

"He is French?" Martínez asked casually.

"He was. He is a man of the People."

Martínez gave a sigh, and tried another approach.

"Are there other men of the People who are French?"

"Only one. Woodchuck. He is married to a woman of the People, also."

"And you learned to speak French from these two men?"

"Oh no. I lived among the French for several winters. That is how I met my husband."

Díaz and Martínez exchanged glances. Now they were making progress.

"Ah yes," the captain almost purred. "And where was this?"

"Oh, far away, Captain. A whole season's travel, up the Great River."

"Then how did Sky-Eyes come to the country of your people?"

"He led a journey there, looking for a way to the Big Water. He did not go back."

The captain looked to Díaz again. This could be significant.

"How many in the party? The others went back?"

"No, no. There were only Sky-Eyes, Woodchuck, and me. One other man, who was killed in an accident."

"A very small party," Martínez observed, a trifle cynically. "When was this?"

"Six, seven winters, maybe."

"And you know of no other such parties?"

"No. The People have seen no others."

"Ah yes. And where, *madame*, is the nearest French post that you know of?"

"Mishi-ghan, where I told you. Beyond the Big River."

"No other?"

"No, Captain."

"Tell me, then, why do you come here?"

"To trade. We need medicine knives."

"Medicine knives?"

"Yes. Knives, lance points, arrowheads of iron. We have none, except one or two. Medicine knives."

"Why not trade with your husband's people?"

"It is too far. You are much closer."

Martínez pondered for a short while.

"You know," he observed, "that I could have you confined or killed? Why should I not do that, in case you are spies?"

Remarkably, the woman smiled again, appearing completely confident.

"Because, Captain, you are an intelligent man. It is to your advantage to help establish trade that will be beneficial to your people and mine."

Martínez once more felt that this woman had been in charge of the entire interview.

"Very well," he said somewhat gruffly. "Please wait outside, *madame*, while we discuss this matter."

She rose, thanked him for his consideration, and Martínez found himself bowing politely and thanking her for coming.

"Lieutenant," he requested, "please escort *Madame* outside, and return at once."

Díaz nodded and turned to the door.

31

» » »

Captain Martínez sat, staring at nothing, and running the entire conversation through his mind. Not once had the woman seemed even uneasy under his questioning. Díaz returned and closed the door.

"Is she not everything I said, Captain?" he smiled.

"Yes, yes, and more, Díaz. But what do we do now? Is she telling the truth?"

"I have felt so, Captain. That, or both she and the man are very skillful liars."

Martínez looked up sharply, surprised at himself. That was a possibility he had all but rejected. In fact, he had become almost defensive about it.

"I think not, Lieutenant. What would they have to gain by it? They do have a prime quality of goods."

He pointed to the pelt on his desk.

"I am inclined to accept their story," he said cautiously, watching to see the reaction of Díaz. "Now, the question is, what do we do with this information?"

"That is your decision, señor. But, I can see that to refer them on up the command might lead them to exploitation."

"Yes, it could happen," agreed the captain. "It might be better for them if we are the ones through which they deal. Better for us, too, of course."

Díaz nodded.

"Or worse, if they are spies."

Martínez looked sharply at him.

"Yes, there is risk, if we are wrong. Do you think it could be worth the risk, Lieutenant?"

"Yes, Captain, I think so, if you agree."

"Very well. We handle it at this level, then. Tell me, is there a trader we can trust?"

"Yes, Gutierrez will treat them fairly. He will pay us a small commission for our support."

"Good, Díaz, this could be very big."

"Or very bad, sir. But I think not. I am satisfied with their story."

"I, too, Díaz. Now, release Sky-Eyes, bring him here to talk of our decision. Bring the woman, too. Then, you go with them to see Gutierrez. Make certain they are satisfied with their trades. This is most important, this first trip here to trade. They must want to return. Now go."

Díaz turned and left the room. He was elated. He saw no possibility that the would-be traders were other than what they seemed. He hurried to the cell block and motioned to the jailer.

"Señor Sky-Eyes!" he called. "Come, I will take you to your wife. The Captain wishes to talk with you both."

They joined Pale Star and the three entered the Captain's office, Sky-Eyes completely confused by this turn of events.

"Señor Sky-Eyes, I have talked with your wife," began Martínez.

Sky-Eyes looked at Star, apparently wondering how this could have taken place with her meager knowledge of Spanish.

"She speaks excellent French," the captain continued with a smile. "Now, about the trading. Lieutenant Díaz will take you to a trader's store, a man called Gutierrez. He will see that you receive fair trade. Only," he cautioned, "each time you come back, contact me or Lieutenant Díaz. Then you will be under our protection. Understood?"

Sky-Eyes nodded.

"We thank you for your help, señor."

"It is nothing," Martínez dismissed the thanks with a wave. "Good luck on your return journey. May we expect you next year?"

"Perhaps," Sky-Eyes agreed cautiously. "We will consider it."

Captain Martínez turned to Pale Star and spoke in French.

"Madame, it has been a pleasure to make your acquaintance."

He bowed gallantly.

"Thank you, *monsieur,"* she smiled.

The three returned to the plaza, where their impatient companions waited. Again, they were drawing some unwanted attention from the sundry loafers around the square. This time, however, the interlopers were prevented from overt contact by the presence of Díaz' troopers.

"Tell them to follow us," Díaz called as he ordered the platoon to mount.

The procession moved down a side street and the lieutenant halted before a squat adobe building with an assortment of goods in evidence along the narrow promenade. Boxes and barrels stood piled against the adobe wall.

Díaz spoke to the sergeant.

"Villa, you may dismiss the platoon. But you stay. I may need your help."

Sergeant Villa barked the commands and the lancers clattered back toward the center of the town. Díaz briefly explained the situation to the sergeant, as the proprietor emerged from his store to see what all the activity was about.

"Ah, good morning, señor! May I be of help?" Gutierrez smiled.

He was of medium height, pleasantly plump, and swarthy of skin. His smile showed even white teeth, and the wrinkles burned into his face by the sun were those of someone with a pleasant disposition.

"You have brought traders?" he asked, noticing the packhorse and its cargo.

"Yes, my friend. These are people from the far plains. They are to be treated as friends of Captain Martínez. This is Sky-Eyes, who speaks our tongue. His wife."

He indicated those of whom he spoke.

"And this," he told the outsiders, "is Señor Enrico Gutierrez. He should have all the 'medicine knives' you need."

Gutierrez was examining the packs.

"They have not brought much to trade," he observed to Díaz.

"These are only samples, señor," Sky-Eyes explained. "If our journey goes well, we will return next season with a bigger train."

"Ah yes," nodded Gutierrez. "Come, I will help you unload."

His eagerness to see the quality of their goods was apparent. He was, however, unprepared for the beauty of the furs when Sky-Eyes opened the first pack. Fox, otter, beaver, mink, badger, raccoon. Even Díaz had not yet seen their display, except for an individual pelt or two.

Propriety dictated, however, that Gutierrez be quite cool and nonchalant.

"Yes, they are acceptable," he murmured, half to himself.

"They are better than that, Gutierrez," pressed the lieutenant. "Come on, accept their worth."

Gutierrez appeared hurt.

"Of course, señor. They are magnificent. But you must allow the trading first!"

"Forgive me, my friend. It is only that the captain wishes that these people be treated with extra fairness."

"We cannot bargain?"

"Of course. But with honor."

"Certainly, Lieutenant. Would I do otherwise?"

The trader still seemed mildly offended.

"Look, Gutierrez, go ahead. Sergeant Villa and I will remain here but we will not interfere."

Now the trading began in earnest.

"What do you wish, Señor Sky-Eyes?" Gutierrez inquired. "Supplies? Flour and meal?"

"No, no. Our needs are different. Knives, lance points, maybe arrow points."

"Yes. I see. Perhaps iron to make these things?"

"No, I think not. We have no smiths."

"Of course. Your people use only stone weapons?"

"Except for one or two. Like this."

The French belt knife slid smoothly out of its scabbard. Gutierrez nodded.

"Yes, señor. I can supply such things. The lance and arrow points, however . . . lance points, perhaps. Arrow points, you could make easily. Let me show you."

32

» » »

The discussion continued, the bargaining and trading. By the time they reached the last of the buffalo robes, shadows were becoming long, and the people of the prairie were beginning to feel closed in by the sunbaked adobe of the town. It seemed important to escape the confines of civilization and return to open country.

It appeared impractical, however. The campsite they had used before was some distance away, and with darkness falling, there would not be time to reach it and establish a camp. Lean Bear and the others cast anxious glances at the lowering sun.

"What is the matter?" Díaz inquired.

Sky-Eyes attempted to explain as best he could.

"It is as I told you. There is a feeling, like a trap, a need to escape to the open under the sky." He paused and smiled. "I even feel it myself sometimes."

"I see. Look, why not leave your goods here at Gutierrez' for the night? It would be difficult to load in the dark. We will show you a place to camp near town, and you can pack in the morning."

Sky-Eyes thought for a moment, then nodded.

"Yes, that is good. Señor Gutierrez wishes to show me something about making arrow points, and he can do that in the morning also."

The trading was finished, and Sergeant Villa and the lieutenant escorted the traders to a nearby campsite near a little stream.

"I will come in the morning to see you off," Díaz promised.

It was pleasant to camp in secure surroundings, under the protection of the Spanish, and without the responsibility of the packs of furs and robes. The night was crisp and clear, the stars appearing near enough to touch against their black velvet. There was a mountain chill in the air, a promise of frost soon. They would have none too much time to travel.

Sky-Eyes and Star walked a little way from the camp.

"It is good, my husband," Star murmured, using now the tongue of the People. "The trading has gone well, no?"

She slipped an arm around his waist.

"Yes, I think so," he responded. "What did you tell them?"

"The truth. That you and Woodchuck are men of the People now. They wanted to know of other French."

"You told them we were French?"

"They knew that. They wanted to know about French, so I told them my own story."

Sky-Eyes laughed aloud. How clever, to distract her questioners from their interest in his background by relating hers. Apparently, it had been successful.

"You told them how far it is to Mishi-ghan?"

"Yes, a whole season's journey, I said."

"It is good! Tell me, Star, can these men be trusted?"

Sky-Eyes felt confident in his own mind, but knew that his wife was an experienced trader, whose skills included estimating the honesty of people. In addition, he knew that somehow a woman has a feel for such things, a judgment beyond the instincts of mere men.

"Yes, I think so," she answered confidently. "I do not know the ways of the Spanish, but these seem good enough. They help themselves by helping us, of course."

"And Gutierrez?"

"Yes, him too. He wants us to come back."

"Star, does your medicine seem good?"

They had occasionally talked of this. Pale Star, with the blood of great medicine men and powerful women in her veins, had had the potential. Looks Far had seen her as an apt student of his art when she was yet a child. "She has the gift," he had told her parents.

Then the girl had been kidnapped, carried off and sold, changed hands until she had come to womanhood far away, among people other than her own.

Her medicine, while not forgotten, had been put aside for a few years. Perhaps, however, it had assisted her to survive, to return to her own People. She had surmounted difficulties that would have felled a lesser spirit. The death of her first husband, her survival with Sky-Eyes after the canoe accident, and their eventual love had all been under the influence, perhaps, of her medicine guide. But her own lodge, her children, continued to interfere.

It was no matter. She could be a medicine woman someday. There were those who believed it better to wait until the uncleanness of menstruation was past, anyway. Meanwhile, she made no effort to accept or refuse the unasked-for gifts of the medicine spirit. Only, sometimes she listened to the wordless advice of the spirit-feeling.

It was of this that her husband now asked her. He had learned that when Star's intuition, or hunches, or . . . well, her *medicine* was unfavorable, it was time to look carefully at their present plans, and to consider changes.

She looked at him in the starlight.

"Yes," she said hesitantly, "I think so. Good, for the trading and for our success. There is still something . . . I do not know, Sky-Eyes. A dark thing, a bad spirit or sign of some sort."

"Why did you not say so?"

"It is not that strong. *Aiee,* sometimes I wish I could see these things better. Looks Far could teach me, I think."

"Yes, he has told me so. You have the gift. But, that is no matter now. Do you feel danger?"

"Yes, some. Not from these soldiers. I think not from the trader."

"From others? From danger on the trail?"

"Maybe. But different than with the danger from the real-cat. I do not know, Sky-Eyes."

"But, Star, Looks Far said we would be successful."

"True, but he mentioned danger, too."

"You think there is more, ahead?"

She was silent a little while. Finally, she spoke, slowly and seriously.

"Yes, I think so. Something we do not yet know about. We must be especially careful."

They watched the Seven Hunters wheel around the Real-Star in the north for a while, as they huddled together in the warmth of a blanket. Finally, they rose and walked back toward the camp, to wake Turkey Foot for the next watch.

For an instant, Sky-Eyes thought he heard a sound among the rocks on the slope. He paused to listen, but it was not repeated.

"What is it?" asked Star.

Sky-Eyes listened a moment longer.

"Nothing, I guess. It was only the horses. They are restless tonight."

33

» » »

The rest of the night proved uneventful. The traders rose with the sun, ate some dried meat and the corn tortillas that seemed a staple of diet in these parts. Still early, they returned to Gutierrez' store.

"Ah, *buenos días*," the trader greeted. "Come, I will show you about the arrow points."

He led Sky-Eyes and Crow to a forge behind the building, where a hot bed of coals already burned. The others followed along. A boy of perhaps ten winters pumped the bellows to encourage the white-hot glow.

"But we have no forge, no anvil," protested Sky-Eyes.

"I know," Gutierrez agreed, "but you have stones?"

"Of course."

"Then select one for an anvil, and build a fire nearby. It will be hot enough. Use hot woods. You have those."

"Yes. There are some trees that will make a hotter fire than others."

The bow-wood, he thought. It makes many sparks, but very hot coals that last a long time.

"Now, take a rod of this iron, or any piece of iron, and put it in the hottest of the coals. It must be nearly white hot."

He lifted an iron bar as thick as a finger, which had been heating in the forge already, placed it on the anvil, and swung his hammer. Sparks flew, and with only a few blows the trader had flattened the tip of the iron rod.

"See? It can be made flat, like the flint used for arrow points."

Gutierrez reheated and continued to shape the point, making a narrower portion to be used as a shank for fastening to the arrow.

"You can make any size or shape you need," he stated, dipping the hot end of the rod in a bucket of water, and holding it up for inspection.

Crow touched the arm of Sky-Eyes.

"But Sky-Eyes, it is not sharp," he protested.

Sky-Eyes translated, and Gutierrez nodded.

"Yes, that is true. You must hammer the edges very thin, and then sharpen by rubbing on a stone, after the point is fastened to the arrow."

This was explained to Crow, who now nodded in turn.

"I see. Like sharpening a bone point. But how does he cut it off the iron stick so it can be used?"

Translation proceeded again.

"I will show you," Gutierrez stated.

He placed the point in the forge once more, and spoke a few words to his young helper. The boy grasped the rod, ready to do his part. Gutierrez picked up another instrument, a heavy chisel. When the time was right, he spoke.

"Now!"

The youngster pulled the hot rod from the forge and held it with the tip lying on the anvil. Gutierrez struck quickly with the hammer and chisel, one, two, three blows, and the newly made arrow point dropped, still smoking, to the ground.

"*Aiee*," exclaimed Crow, fascinated. "I see how it is done!"

Gutierrez picked up the hot arrow point with tongs and quenched it in his water bucket. Then he handed it to Sky-Eyes, who examined it and handed it on to Lean Bear.

"Now all you really need are the hammer and a chisel," Gutierrez assured them, "and some iron, of course."

He held up the slender iron rod.

Crow spoke aside to Sky-Eyes.

"The medicine stone can only be shaped or cut with another piece of medicine stone!" he said slowly, in wonder.

"Yes, maybe so," Sky-Eyes agreed.

He had not thought of it in just those terms.

"Ask him, Sky-Eyes, if I may try."

Gutierrez readily agreed. It would be greatly to his benefit if he could establish continuous trade with these people of the plains. He watched the efforts of Lean Bear, clumsy at first but gaining confidence.

"You can use a broken knife, a sword, anything of iron to make arrow points," he offered.

Sky-Eyes was thinking along other lines.

"Are lance points made the same way?"

"Yes. They are more difficult, the balance, because of the length. They must be straight and true. I am not very good at this, señor, only enough to show you, but it is done in the same way, the more difficult things."

"Knives? The same way?"

The possession of the medicine knife was the start of this entire improbable adventure, he was recalling. It was the knife that he felt was important. Lance points, even arrows, were used seldom, but a knife was called upon every day, for everyday uses like eating.

Gutierrez chuckled at the question.

"That involves other things, señor," he explained patiently. "Better steel, different treatment. You could make a knife of this," he picked up the iron rod, "but it would never hold an edge. It could not be tempered. But I do not know of such things."

He spread his hands helplessly.

"Come, I will help you pack," he offered.

The rest of the party had been standing near the doorway of the building, watching from a safe distance. The noise and the showers of sparks that flew from the medicine fire were disconcerting. By this time, however, they had relaxed somewhat. It appeared that the forge was under a certain degree of control, and they had begun to revert to more normal behavior. Star had stepped inside to begin assembling the packs.

Turkey Foot was squatting near the entrance, chewing on a chunk of pemmican.

"What is he eating?" Gutierrez asked.

"Dried meat," Sky-Eyes replied. "No, pemmican."

"What is it?"

"Dried meat, pounded and mixed with buffalo fat. Sometimes they put berries in it."

"But how do you carry such stuff?"

"It is put in the intestine of a buffalo, to store or to carry."

"Like sausages?"

"Well, yes."

He had not thought of it in that way.

"Does this . . . 'pemmican' keep well?"

"Yes. Not as well as dried meat, but well enough. Here, try it."

He turned and requested a bite of the pemmican from Turkey Foot, who handed over a small chunk.

"I am sorry, Sky-Eyes, that is the last of it."

"It is all right. Gutierrez only wishes to taste it."

The trader chewed thoughtfully.

"Yes," he mused. "You use this for traveling supplies?"

"Only some. Dried meat is more useful, and less weight."

"Of course."

The trader was absorbed in thought.

Amigo," he said finally, "when you come back, could you bring dried meat and some of this?"

"Yes, maybe so. The meat, surely. The pemmican will not keep well if the weather is too hot. You wish to trade for these things?"

The trader grinned broadly.

"Gutierrez will trade for anything!" he proclaimed. "But, I think this might be good to try."

Star had already begun wrapping and tying the bundles of their newly acquired goods. These packs would be small but heavy, compared to the bulky fluff of the furs and robes. It would be necessary to pad the packs carefully, to prevent gouging the horse with any of the various iron implements as the loads shifted during travel.

It did not take long. The pack horse was ready, and they wished to cover much distance by nightfall. They were distrustful of the weather, in an unfamiliar area, and with autumn approaching rapidly.

True to his word, Díaz came to see them off.

"We will expect you next season," he said as he shook hands with Sky-Eyes in farewell.

"Perhaps," agreed Sky-Eyes cautiously. "We still have half our journey ahead of us."

"Yes, but now the trail is known to you."

He bowed gallantly to Pale Star.

"*Madame*, it has been a pleasure to make your acquaintance," he spoke in French.

"Thank you, *monsieur*, and for all your help."

Díaz turned back to Sky-Eyes.

"May I offer an escort of troopers the first day?"

Sky-Eyes was startled.

"Why? Do you expect danger to us?"

"No, no," assured Díaz. "Only as an honor guard."

Sky-Eyes considered only a moment.

"No, Lieutenant, I think not. It is good for our people to be alone in the open again. But we thank you for the honor."

He swung to the saddle and the party moved down the street toward the trail. Star rode alongside.

"What did the lieutenant say at the last, there? I understood only a word or two. Something about soldiers?"

"Yes, he offered us protection. An escort."

"He expects danger to us?"

"I think not. It is more of an honor."

They rode on in silence for a little way.

Why, then, Sky-Eyes was thinking, why do I wonder? And why does Star seem to have some concern over it? What is her medicine trying to tell her?

34

» » »

The trading party traveled well, now more familiar with the trail. After an adjustment or two, the new packs seemed to be no problem. It was a matter of balance, Sky-Eyes realized. Much like loading a canoe in the lake country or on a river journey. Keep an equal weight on each side, and the bulk of the load low, to avoid overbalancing. The pack horse soon adjusted to the change, from a large bulky load to a smaller, heavy burden of iron bars and steel weapons.

"The trading went well, I think," Sky-Eyes observed to his wife.

They were riding side by side on this open portion of the trail. The occasional touch of a knee as their horses moved closer together for a moment was a comforting thing. They had endured much concern for each other's safety during their worrisome stay in Santa Fe. It had been difficult to be apart, as it always was for them, but more especially with the threat of the unknown prominent in their minds. It was good to be together again, traveling in the open. In unfamiliar terrain, to be sure, but at least headed for the big skies of the prairie country.

Star had not answered his comment, and he looked at her quizzically.

"Do you not think so?" he pressed.

"What? Oh yes, Sky-Eyes, the trading, yes."

"Then what?"

"I do not know."

"Is there something wrong?"

"No. Something is just not quite right."

"I do not understand, Star."

"No do I, my husband. There is just a feeling."

"Your medicine?"

"Maybe."

"Let us talk, then. Does it seem to be about the lieutenant, Díaz? Or the captain? Both, maybe?"

His tone was urgent.

"No," she said slowly. "I am made to think they mean well."

"Then the trader, Gutierrez. Is he not to be trusted?"

Star gave a deep sigh.

"No, no, Sky-Eyes, I think he tries to help us. But you know how it is with my medicine. There is just a feeling, I cannot tell."

She paused and thought a moment.

"The feel for the trip, the trading, is good," she continued, "but something unseen, something we have not yet seen."

"You mean like enemies?"

"Well, yes. But we have no enemies here. We have eaten with the mud-lodge people."

To have shared a meal was a significant alliance, a meeting of spirits. One cannot share the food of another without becoming closer, eliminating many possible controversies because their spirits have shared sustenance.

"Yes, it is not the mud-lodge people."

"Then who else is there? Other tribes?"

An unpleasant feeling prickled along the back of his neck. Was there some place-spirit here, or on their route back, that would be intolerant toward them? Could it be, even, that the People were not intended to have the medicine knives. Was this like the Jews, with their strange taboos about eating the flesh of pigs?

Ridiculous, the civilized portion of his mind told him. Such things are superstition. Close on the heels of that thought came the realization of the accuracy of Pale Star's hunches, her medicine feelings. The uncanny predictions of

Looks Far, who seemed to see things not seen by others. Things of the spirit.

"Other tribes? Maybe." Star was saying. "I do not know."

The trail narrowed, around the shoulder of one of the foothills that would have seemed a mountain, closer to home. They resumed a single file, skirting the steep slope, the trail crawling snakelike around each rise. Footing for the horses was more unsure, and their pace became necessarily slower. Ahead of them in the distance stretched the blue of more mountains. It would be better, Sky-Eyes thought, after they crossed the pass. Then they could at least see the promise of the plains to the east as they traveled north along the front range. It would be good to reach the Red Rocks band, and prepare for the winter with them. He wondered how the children were faring with Woodchuck and Yellow Head. It would be good to see them, too.

"Turkey Foot! Sky-Eyes!" came a call from the rear of the column. "We are followed!"

Sky-Eyes turned to look back. Lean Bear was pointing. There, on a fairly level stretch of plain some distance away, a column of riders could be seen. He rode back to a better vantage point and dismounted, Star and Turkey Foot close beside him.

"Soldiers?" someone asked.

"No," observed Sky-Eyes. "See, they ride loosely in no formation. There is no spacing like that of soldiers."

"Ah yes. Natives?" asked Lean Bear.

They watched a little longer.

"No," decided Turkey Foot. "I think not. They must be Hairfaces."

Sky-Eyes raised his hands, curled his fists into a long tube to look through, after the manner of the plains tribes. He was always surprised at how the image of distant objects was clarified by shutting out the surrounding light. He watched the riders a moment. Ten, no, eleven, he counted. In a fight, they would be badly outnumbered. True, there was no indication that a fight was imminent, but it must remain a possibility. They must look for terrain favorable to defense.

The riders were moving rapidly. They must necessarily slow when they reached the hilly part of the trail, but they were coming. If the strangers were indeed pursuing them, they could probably overtake the little trading party by dark. It would be impossible to travel by night in unfamiliar mountain country. They must camp, and the riders behind them would have the entire night to creep up in assault.

It was essential, then, to look for a defensible campsite well before dark, to become established. He tried to remember such a place on the journey in, but none came to mind.

"Look!" Lean Bear exclaimed suddenly. "The fat one near the front. We have seen him before!"

The others spoke in agreement.

"Where?" Sky-Eyes asked, confused. "I do not remember."

"In the plaza," Star told him. "They crowded around us, tried to untie the packs. That is why we left."

"These are the same ones?"

"I think so. It is as Bear says, the fat one. He is their leader, maybe."

So, thought Sky-Eyes. Spaniards but not soldiers. Renegades, perhaps. They could be dangerous. And they would know that the travelers carried goods recently traded for.

"The fat one wanted Star, too," observed Lean Bear matter-of-factly.

"What?"

"Yes," agreed Star. "I would have said nothing, but it is true."

The fat one, Sky-Eyes thought, has not seen her in combat. He has much to learn. He thought of the time they had fought a group of scalp-hunters in Mishi-ghan, before they had found love. They were outnumbered then, too.

Star interrupted his thoughts.

"This may be my medicine-feeling, Sky-Eyes," she mused.

They mounted and continued on the trail, watching to the rear and also on the lookout for a place to camp and defend.

Star spoke once more.

"Yes, this must be it. I think we will fight."

35

» » »

It was midafternoon now, and they had not yet selected a place to camp. From time to time they caught a glimpse of their pursuers in the distance. The other horsemen had shortened the distance between them until they reached the more mountainous region of the trail. Since then, they had not gained at all.

"Could it be," questioned Sky-Eyes, "that this is only another party following the same trail?"

Everyone chuckled, and then realized that he was serious.

"I think not, Sky-Eyes," Turkey Foot offered. "You did not see these men, as we did in the plaza. They are bad medicine."

The others nodded agreement.

"Besides, my medicine tells me," added Pale Star.

"So be it," admitted Sky-Eyes. "Then we will have to fight them. But we choose the place."

Sometime later Turkey Foot suddenly pointed ahead.

"Look!"

A flattopped mesa lay ahead. Or rather, stood ahead. Tall and straightsided, it was one of the prominent features of the area.

"I had forgotten," Turkey Foot continued. "I was told that it was the home of the Old Ones. See, their lodges?"

It was possible, as they drew closer, to see the ruins of a number of buildings on the top of the mesa. They appeared much like the mud-lodges of Blue Corn's people. There also appeared several caves just below the rim of the cliff. Some had been improved as dwellings by building an adobe wall to enclose the natural caves and rock formations.

Sky-Eyes was startled that they had not seen this evidence of an older civilization on the incoming journey. Then he realized that the ruins could only be seen from this direction. They had not had occasion to look back, on the incoming journey.

Now he could see the practical defensive advantage to the cliff dwellers, the Old Ones. Those people, whoever they were, had undoubtedly had enemies. Anyone intent on doing them harm would have to approach one at a time. Now he could see the trail as it zigzagged along the steep face of the cliff. A child could defend against any potential attacker, merely by standing at the top and tossing rocks over the rim at the climbers. In some places, steps and handholds had been cut in the rock to assist in the more vertical portions of the climb.

If they could achieve that position, they could defend themselves against those who followed. They had all drunk their fill at the last stream they encountered, and watered the horses.

Aiee! Sky-Eyes thought. The horses! They could not take horses up that precipice. If they left them below, their pursuers would take them, and the party would be on foot.

"Turkey Foot," he asked, "is there another way up the mesa?"

"I do not know. Usually two paths, I think."

"Then the other has to be easier than this. Look. There are big tree trunks in those lodges. They could not be carried up this side."

"I will ride ahead and see if I can find it."

He touched heels to his mare and was gone, circling the cliff at its base. There was none too much time. If they could reach the mesa's top before dark, and before their pursuers discovered their plan . . . It was possible, even, that if their location was not discovered, those who followed them might give up. Sky-Eyes immediately dismissed that thought as wishful thinking.

Turkey Foot was out of sight now, around the shoulder of

the bluff. It was time to make a move, yet they did not yet know what that move should be.

"Come," Sky-Eyes called, reining his horse off the trail. "We will meet Turkey Foot at the cliff's base."

They kept looking back, but as yet there was no sign of the enemy. Then a shout came from almost directly overhead.

"Sky-Eyes! Bear! Come on around the hill!"

Turkey Foot was standing at the edge of the precipice, looking down on them.

"The trail is good!" he added. The others quickly followed his direction, pushing the horses to reach the shelter of the mesa. They were none too soon. Sky-Eyes, riding in the rear, glanced back, just before he rounded the corner, to see moving specks appear in the distance along the back trail.

The climb was steep but uncomplicated. The trail had not been made for horses, but it was possible to use them, riding most of the way. The last few paces they found it necessary to dismount and lead the animals up the rocky slope. Turkey Foot waited at the top.

"This will be easy to defend," he offered. "Only at this point and the one on the other side could the hill be climbed."

"It is good!" agreed Sky-Eyes.

The top of the mesa was perhaps one long bow shot wide and two or three long, perfectly flat and level. At one end clustered the ruined pueblos, and at the other there was a little winter-cured grass for the horses.

"What about water?" someone asked.

"We must save what we have," Turkey Foot advised. "Maybe this will be over before our need becomes great."

No one answered, but everyone was thinking the same thing. They had placed themselves in a defensive position that was completely impregnable. However, in doing so, perhaps they had created a trap for themselves. It might be impossible to get off of the mesa. The enemy had only to wait. Sooner or later the siege would end when food and water ran out. They would have to try to fight their way down, or die of starvation and thirst.

These gloomy thoughts were interrupted by a soft call from Beaver Tooth who had gone to look from the precipice.

"Look! They come!" he beckoned.

The others rushed to join him, taking cover behind boulders at the rim. Sky-Eyes crouched low, Star at his elbow. Cautiously, they peered over the edge.

The first glimpse was breathtaking. They were looking down on the tops of scattered trees, which looked small from above but were actually sizable pines. In the distance, several hundred paces away, the trail wandered along the base of the hills. And on the trail, riding in a loose column, came their pursuers.

Now they were nearing the point where Sky-Eyes had led his party off the trail. Everyone watched expectantly. It was possible that the riders would pass on down the trail. If so, with night coming on, it might be possible to evade a confrontation, though in his heart, Sky-Eyes knew better.

The riders moved on without pausing, perhaps fifty paces, and then stopped. There was argument, and pointing to the trail, both ahead and behind. One rider swung away from the group and rode back slowly, studying the ground.

The story was all too plain. The riders had realized that their quarry was no longer in front of them! There were no fresh hoofprints on the trail ahead. The swarthy man who rode slowly back was a tracker, looking for the spot where they had left the path. If there had been any doubt as to the intentions of the pursuing party, this eliminated it entirely.

The tracker stopped and pointed to the ground with a shout, and the others hurried to join him. There was a brief discussion, and one of the men pointed to the top of the cliff. This seemed to stimulate the entire group to action. Those who had dismounted swung to their saddles, and the entire party loped in a disorganized melee toward the mesa.

"*Aiee!*" whispered Turkey Foot. "They come!"

36

» » »

The riders came to a sliding stop directly below where Sky-Eyes crouched. The one who appeared to be their leader seemed to study the situation for a little while.

"Hello!" he shouted, though the listeners were still unseen. "Do any of you speak Spanish?"

There was no longer any need to hide. Sky-Eyes rose from behind the boulder, and there was a murmur of talk from below. The fat man motioned them to silence.

"Who wishes to know?" Sky-Eyes called.

"Ah, *amigo,* this is good. Come down, we will camp together and talk."

"No, we have already made camp," Sky-Eyes answered.

"Very well, we will come up and join you."

"No! What do you want?"

"You are traders," the fat one called back. "We wish to trade."

"Our trading is finished. And, we plainly see that you carry no trade goods."

The fat man appeared angry for a moment, then his tone became oily.

"I see, *amigo,* that I cannot deceive you. Look, we make our poor living by extracting toll from travelers. You have not yet paid the toll."

"And will not!" Sky-Eyes shouted back. "We have dealt with the Señor Gutierrez and our trading is finished. There will be no talk of toll."

147

"This is unwise, señor!" The fat one answered. "Before this is over, you will wish you had been easier to deal with."

He paused a moment, and then continued.

"Look, it is plain that while we cannot come up, you also cannot come down. Your food and water will be gone, and you will die. Then we will have all your goods. I do not wish that to happen."

"Then what do you propose?"

"Send the woman down. She can warm our beds for one night, and then you can be on your way, no worse off than before."

Sky-Eyes held back his anger and managed a laugh.

"Surely you are joking, señor. What would you know of how to treat a woman of quality? It would serve you right, though, if I sent her down. I have seen her kill better men than you for less!"

The fat man became furious.

"You are in no position to talk so!" he yelled. "We will kill you all and take the woman."

Sky-Eyes saw that he had touched a sensitive point. If he could work on the man's anger, perhaps he could goad him to irrational action.

"Your mother eats dung, Fat Man!" he shouted. "Worms will crawl in and out of your eye sockets before such a thing happens! Coyotes will gnaw your bones!"

"You will regret this!" screamed the other. "You will beg for death to come!"

"Ha!" Sky-Eyes yelled back. "Does the worm threaten the eagle? Go and crawl back in your dung heap!"

"What is happening?" demanded Lean Bear. "Tell us!"

"He demands tribute," explained Sky-Eyes quickly. "Our goods."

He decided not to mention about Star to the others.

Star said nothing, but her husband saw a flicker of a smile across her face. He had come to know that as a dangerous look. Perhaps she understood more Spanish than he realized.

"When the time comes to fight, the fat one is mine!" she stated with finality.

The others chuckled. The fat one was not in an enviable position.

Lean Bear rose, fitted an arrow to his bow, and let it fly. The missile floated out over the void, arched down, and struck harmlessly in the ground, far short of the riders below. They laughed in disdain.

"Save your arrows, Bear," advised Turkey Foot. "It is too hard to judge distance with so long a drop."

"I know," Lean Bear admitted. "But I want them to know the Bear is here."

"Bear," said Turkey Foot suddenly, "how many did you count on the trail?"

"Eleven, I think."

"But there are only ten. Where is the other one?"

Lean Bear turned quickly and looked across the level plateau. Just then one of the horses raised its head and whinnied. Bear and Turkey Foot, weapons ready, sprinted toward the head of the trail. It was all too apparent now. While the main party of their pursuers had confronted Sky-Eyes, one had circled the mesa to come up the back trail.

They reached the point where the last steep narrow section of the trail came over the rim and onto the plateau, to find nothing. There was no creeping assailant coming up the trail, no horse.

"There is no one here," Turkey Foot called.

The others relaxed. Lean Bear trotted back across the open flat.

"Turkey Foot will take the watch now."

"It is good," agreed Sky-Eyes. "Should we have two at the back trail?"

"I think not. One at each trail."

Shadows were lengthening. They must establish camp, and select places to sleep. No one even considered the dubious shelter of the ruined pueblos. The people of the prairie chose a spot in the open without a thought.

The late autumn twilight was all too brief, and darkness descended over the mesa. The mandatory camp fire came to life, shedding a tiny circle of light in the vastness of the mountain country. Fuel was scarce, but the symbolism of the occasion was carried out, even for a brief time.

Sky-Eyes relieved Crow for the second watch at the head of the steep climb up the cliff's face. Star joined him, bringing some dried meat and some of the parched corn they had obtained from the trader. The two sat against a sunwarmed boulder, sharing a robe around their shoulders.

Far below, two points of light sparkled to show the camp of the renegades. It was a peaceful enough scene, the mesa and the plain below faintly lit by dim starlight. Only the knowledge of the danger they faced contradicted the peace of the quiet night. In the distance, a coyote called, and another answered.

After a while Star left him to get some sleep. Nothing had been said, but Sky-Eyes was certain that she knew about the demands made by their assailants. His anger rose when he thought of it. He actually found himself looking forward to the coming fight. His only concern was that they were badly outnumbered. That was offset, of course, by the fact that their assailants could only attack one at a time. Two, actually, one by each trail. Close behind would be another, and yet another.

His thoughts drifted to the original inhabitants of the mesa, the Old Ones. He felt very close to them tonight. Surely their spirits walked among the ruins of their homes. He could feel the kinship of those whose moccasined feet had worn the path in front of him, inches deep in solid stone. He wondered how many generations it had taken to wear that path over the rim.

What had happened to the Old Ones? No one was sure. Had there come a time when their fortresslike town was besieged by an enemy? Did a sentry sit, as Sky-Eyes now sat, guarding the head of the path and waiting for the attack that must come?

Back to the present, he decided that the renegades would make at least one try to overcome them before settling down to wait. They must do that to save face. If he were planning an attack on such a stronghold, he thought, it would be two-pronged. Front and back, at the same time.

Yes, that would be what their attackers would do, he decided. And as for timing, there was no question. Darkness would allow them to bring several men into position, or nearly so. Then they would attack when the defenders were heavy with sleep. Yes, surely the attack would come at dawn.

37

» » »

Pale Star relieved him for the next watch when the Seven Hunters showed the night more than half gone. They talked a moment, and he told her of his suspicion of the dawn attack.

"I think you are right, Sky-Eyes. Yes, you should go and tell the others."

He nodded.

"Yes, I will tell them. And, I will come back here."

"But you must rest."

"Yes, of course. But I want to be with you when morning comes. I will come back and sleep here."

She circled his waist with a brief hug.

"It is good, my husband."

He found Lean Bear at the other watch point, and explained his idea. Lean Bear nodded.

"I will be careful."

Sky-Eyes sought out the others and told them also, and then returned to Star. He rolled in his sleeping robe but sleep would not come. The coming excitement made him restless, and he tossed fitfully. Finally, he slept.

It was still dark, but graying in the east, when Star roused him.

"Wake up, Sky-Eyes."

He sat up, trying to become alert through the disorientation of waking in a strange place.

"What is it, Star? Are they here?"

"No. Well, yes, I could hear them on the cliff below a little while ago. But this is something else."

"Yes?"

"You remember the missing man? The one we thought might come up the back trail?"

"What about him?"

"I think that one is the tracker, the dark man we saw."

"Maybe. Why?"

"Sky-Eyes, where did he go?"

"Who knows?"

"But we should know. We *must* know."

"Why? What . . . ?"

"We thought he did not reach the top. What if he did? He could hide among the old lodges, and attack someone up here to confuse the ones on watch."

Of course! That was the missing component. A diversionary attack from an unexpected source, followed by the two-pronged attack at the trailheads. Their forces would be spread thin, and outnumbered two to one.

"Star, we must warn them! The sleepers first. Go! I will stay here."

She hurried away. It was growing lighter already, and he moved into position with his lance ready. He heard, or perhaps imagined that he heard, a soft scuffling on the path below the rim. He hesitated to look over the edge. Silhouetted against the paling sky, he would be a target for an arrow. He shivered a little, from cold and excitement and the knowledge that somewhere behind him, still hidden, was an assassin who had spent the night waiting for the right moment to kill.

At that moment came a shout from the area where the camp fire had been. It sounded like Star's voice, but Sky-Eyes had no time to think of that. A dark figure loomed before him, rising over the rim of the cliff. He brought his spear into play, ready for the thrust. There were running footsteps behind him, and for a fraction of a heartbeat, he was distracted. The attacker seized the shaft of the lance just behind the head, and jerked forward.

Off balance, Sky-Eyes almost fell as he fumbled for his belt knife. He was fighting for his life now. The assailant, a large and powerful man, suddenly shifted from the pull on the lance and pushed it backward. Sky-Eyes caught his heel and fell heavily, and in an instant his assailant lunged forward, a diving plunge to land with all his weight. He apparently intended to pin the stunned defender beneath him, using the considerable size of his body to his advantage.

Sky-Eyes, the breath knocked from his lungs by the fall, was gasping like a beached fish, at the same time trying to bring his knife into play. The weapon had barely cleared the sheath when the massive form of the attacker descended. Sky-Eyes saw the glint of a knife in the man's hand, and tried to turn his own blade upward. His own motions seemed slow and futile, dreamlike, while those of his opponent seemed deft and rapid.

The crushing weight of the man's plunge landed squarely on him now, and he grasped with his left hand for the knife-wielding wrist of the other. He felt that he must hold on, his life depended on it. He was no longer certain why, exactly, as his vision grew blacker and breath refused to enter his lungs. Only that he *must* hold on.

Then the powerful muscles of the other man relaxed. The knife dropped to the ground beside Sky-Eyes' shoulder. His assailant gave a convulsive shudder and then became limp. Sky-Eyes was still fighting for breath, confused and frantic with the dead weight on his chest. His right arm was pinned under the weight of the other man. No, that was not it. His mind was playing tricks on him. He still held the haft of his knife in a death grip, and could not move his arm as long as he held that grip. The knife was fastened to something and he could not budge it. Slowly, he began to realize that the attacker had unwittingly thrown himself on the point of the knife as Sky-Eyes drew it from the scabbard and prepared to defend himself.

He was still fighting to free himself from the dead man's weight when a second figure rose in silhouette against the lightening sky, another man climbing over the rim. He could recognize the bulky proportions of the leader of the renegades, the one they had been calling the Fat One. Sky-Eyes desperately fumbled with his left hand for the knife dropped by the dead man. His own knife seemed hopelessly lodged in the belly of the assailant.

The Fat One stepped forward, moving quickly for one of his bulk, and placed his booted foot on Sky-Eyes' searching hand. He stooped and knocked the knife aside, then readied his own for a thrust.

It had all happened so rapidly, and was ending so soon. A phrase from the Death Song of the People flitted through his mind: "Today is a good day to die . . ."

He was aware that the running footsteps behind him had stopped, and he heard the voice of Pale Star. She was yelling at the Fat One, in her own tongue, hurling blistering obscenities. The man could not understand her words, but his attention was distracted. He looked up. Sky-Eyes heard a whirring swish and something struck the man's face. He straightened, jerking convulsively, with Star's throwing-ax jutting from between his eyes. He swayed backward and disappeared over the rim of the cliff.

There was an exclamation from below, and the sound of an impact, and a choked scream as someone else joined the falling body of his leader. It seemed a long time before the sound of a muffled, double thud was heard from far below.

38

» » »

Pale Star rolled the body of the dead attacker from her husband, and helped him to sit up.

"Are you all right?"

"Yes," he gasped, still fighting for breath. "You?"

"Yes."

Turkey Foot came running.

"Are you . . . *aiee!*" he exclaimed.

He stepped to the edge and looked down. The day was rapidly growing light now.

"*Two* more below?" he asked. "We killed two at the other trail, and the one in the old lodges."

"Our people? How many hurt?" Sky-Eyes panted.

"Crow is dead. Lean Bear, an arrow through the arm. He will be all right."

"You are hurt," Star observed, pointing to a crimson stain spreading on the shoulder of his buckskin shirt.

"Only a scratch. It was good you warned us. How did you know? About the one who hid, I mean?"

Sky-Eyes answered for his wife.

"Her medicine," he said simply.

"I did not have time to tell them all," Star explained. "So I yelled."

Turkey Foot looked over the rim again. Voices drifted up from below, talking excitedly.

"Let us give them something else to think about!" he suggested.

He bent and pulled the knife from the corpse, wiped it on the dead man's shirt, and handed it to Sky-Eyes. Then he grasped the lifeless form and with a mighty heave, tossed the erstwhile killer over the edge. Shouts from below brought a grim smile to his face.

"Tell them, Sky-Eyes. Only you know their tongue. Ask them how many they have left."

Sky-Eyes, breathing easier now, struggled to his feet and walked to look over the rim. Far below, the little cluster of survivors looked upward in awe.

"You, below!" Sky-Eyes shouted. "This is how our tribe's enemies are treated."

"Tell them we are coming down after them," suggested Turkey Foot whimsically. "They have only five left."

"But there is no need . . ." began Sky-Eyes.

"Of course not," Star interrupted, "we need not *do* it, just *tell* them we will."

Turkey Foot chuckled, and Sky-Eyes nodded.

"We are coming for the rest of you, now," he shouted.

There was a hurried conference, then a flurry of activity. By the time Sun Boy was completely above earth's rim, the would-be desperadoes were raising dust back along the trail to Santa Fe.

It was many sleeps later that the travelers plodded along the trail northward, nearing the winter camp of the Red Rocks band. There was a bite in the wind today. They had already encountered snow in the mountain passes, a thin blanket of white that had disappeared within a day. They had been concerned about being in a territory where they did not know the seasons. On the familiar prairie, unpredictable though it might be, there was a certain confidence in their approach to the weather. In the mountains . . . *aiee*, the Red Rocks had told them of snow many times deeper than a tall man's height. It was a frightening thing, the unknown spirit of the mountain winter. Cold Maker was said to live in northern mountains, but it was apparent that he came south to challenge Sun Boy's medicine each autumn. They cast anxious glances at the muddy sky and tried to ignore the few flakes of snow that stung their faces out of the north.

"Should we find a shelter and camp?" inquired Sky-Eyes.

"I think not, Sky-Eyes," answered Turkey Foot. "There is not much food for the horses here."

To their left, the long dark ridge of the front range stretched north as far as they could see. Snow already shone on the higher peaks. Time was growing short, and it was growing colder.

"Where do you think the Red Rocks are camped?" Star asked.

"They always stay in nearly the same place," offered Beaver Tooth, the man of that band. "The Rocks are our medicine, you know."

"Yes. Do you know how far?"

Beaver Tooth glanced at the sky.

"Maybe tonight. Not far."

Even so, dusk was settling before they neared the village. Lean Bear suddenly sniffed the wind.

"Smoke!"

Yes, it was distinctly there, a hint of wood smoke in the north wind. Before much longer, they would have had to make some sort of camp for the night. They were becoming chilled now.

"Yes, that will be the village!" Beaver Tooth agreed.

They pushed on, snow coming harder now. Then, in the dusk ahead, an orange-red glow, another, and another. There was no mistaking the light from the night fires glowing through tight-drawn lodge skins. There would be warmth inside. The travelers entered the area among the lodges.

"*Ah-koh!*" shouted Beaver Tooth. "We are home!"

People began to look out of lodge doors, and some came running.

"Sky-Eyes!" shouted Woodchuck, nearly dragging his friend from the horse. "Come into the lodge!"

He assisted in caring for the horses, and the travelers came crowding into the lodge of Woodchuck and Yellow Head. Star spread her arms to her children, and everyone talked at once.

"Tell me, Sky-Eyes," said Woodchuck, aside, "was it a good trip? Did you have any trouble?"

"Only a little," his friend answered, warming himself at the lodge fire.

He was tired, longing to sleep.

"We will tell you all about it," he smiled. "We lost a horse, part of our furs, I spent the night in jail, we fought bandits, and nearly froze coming in."

"But you traded with the Spanish? You saw them?"

"Yes, my friend! We have brought medicine knives, and iron for arrow points. My lance point!"

"It was worth it?"

Sky-Eyes thought for a moment.

"Yes," he mused, "yes, it will be good for the People."

"You think we should go again?"

"Yes. They want us to. Star is excited about it. Only . . . Star, you think we should go back, no?"

Star looked up, smiling happily, her children in her arms.

"Of course!" she agreed. "Only next year, could we go a little earlier in the season? We tempted Cold Maker a little."

GENEALOGY

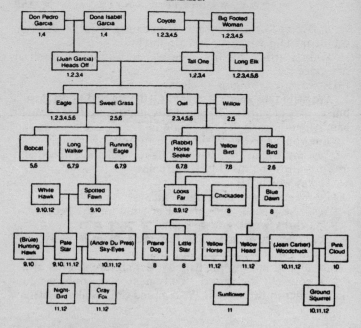

Dates for Volumes in the Spanish Bit Saga

 1 TRAIL OF THE SPANISH BIT — 1540–44
 2 THE ELK-DOG HERITAGE — 1544–45
 3 FOLLOW THE WIND — 1547–48
 4 BUFFALO MEDICINE — 1559–61
 5 MAN OF THE SHADOWS — 1565–66
 6 DAUGHTER OF THE EAGLE — 1583–84
 7 THE MOON OF THUNDER — 1600–01
 8 THE SACRED HILLS — 1625–27
 9 PALE STAR — 1630–31
10 RIVER OF SWANS — 1636–38
11 RETURN TO THE RIVER — 1642–44
12 THE MEDICINE KNIFE — 1650–52

Dates are only approximate, since the People have no written calendar.

Characters in the Genealogy appear in the volumes indicated.

ANNOUNCING A "SUPER" SPANISH BIT
NOVEL BY DON COLDSMITH
FROM BANTAM BOOKS

THE CHANGING WIND

In this magnificent epic tale by the bestselling author of The Spanish Bit Saga, the world of the native people of the Great Plains comes vividly, colorfully to life. It is a world of powerful forces of good and evil, of simple and sometimes dangerous tribal life, it is the world of White Buffalo, the medicine man of the People.

Don Coldsmith has created his largest, most panoramic novel to date with THE CHANGING WIND. Turn the page for a preview of this great novel, which will be on sale in January 1990 wherever Bantam Books are sold.

1

» » »

There was little about the childhood of Small Elk that foretold his place in the story of the People. Perhaps his mother, Dove Woman, anticipated that her son was destined for greatness, but such expectations are regarded as a mother's privilege. However, his father also suspected that here was a child with an unusual mission.

The two older children of Dove Woman and White Buffalo had grown, married, and had their own lodges before the coming of Small Elk to the lodge of the medicine man. That alone set him apart, but there were other things that his father noticed. There was his curiosity. The child would sit for long spaces of time, watching a column of ants going in and out of their underground lodge. There were those in the tribe, White Buffalo knew, who would regard this as useless activity. And, he had to admit, for some it may have been. But not for Small Elk. There was something about the *way* the child watched the creatures. His father was certain that Small Elk *understood* the apparently aimless scurrying around the ant hill. He did not say so, but there was a look of wonder on the small·face, the wonder of learning. White Buffalo saw in the shining dark eyes an understanding of the spirit of the ants.

It was, in a way, like the understanding that had been in the eyes of the infant the day of his birth. White Buffalo had seen many infants. Most were squalling in protest at the indignity of having been thrust from the warm and protective lodge which had been theirs for the past nine moons. True, it was a rude shock to enter a world that included cold and hunger. But occasionally, there would be an infant whose approach to life seemed different. And this was such an infant. After the preliminary protest, and the cough to clear newly-expanded lungs, this child was quiet.

The woman who had assisted Dove Woman with the birth lifted the lodge flap to allow the father to enter and see his son. White Buffalo paused a moment, allowing his eyes to become accustomed to the dim interior of the lodge. He smiled at his wife.

"Our son is here," Dove Woman said softly.

"It is well with you?" he asked.

"Of course. Come, look at him."

She lifted the corner of the robe that covered her. White Buffalo knelt and looked into the small red face. It was only then that he felt the impact of the tiny newcomer. The eyes, which in most infants are squinted tightly shut against the new experience of light and air, were in this case wide open. They looked around the lodge and then directly into his own, with a shocking intensity that startled White Buffalo.

It must be remembered that White Buffalo was no ordinary man in his own right. His medicine was considered strong, his vision accurate. His contact with things of the spirit was an ongoing, vibrant thing. Even so, it was with something of a shock that he looked into the dark eyes of this newborn child. There was knowledge there, and an interest, a curiosity, that burned brightly in those eyes. Unaccountably, White Buffalo felt for an instant that he was the one under scrutiny, not the child. This small one seemed to already possess an understanding of the nature of the world, and a desire to learn more about it.

"This is a strong spirit," he told his wife.

"Of course," Dove Woman smiled. "He is ours, yours and mine."

White Buffalo nodded, still entranced by the strange feeling of communication he had had for a moment. The moment had passed, now.

"Let us call him 'Small Elk'," Dove Woman suggested.

White Buffalo knew that this was because of their experience the evening before. It was exceptionally fine weather, early in the Moon of Roses, and they had walked a little way from the lodges to be alone and enjoy the setting of the sun. Dove Woman had grown large, and was impatient to bring forth her child. It was pleasant to walk with her husband, and to admire the lavish colors of the western sky.

"Sun Boy chooses his paints well this evening," she observed.

"Yes," her husband agreed.

After all their years together, there was little need for talk. They communicated without it, each understanding what the other felt. This evening they were comfortable with each other and with the world. It was a time of waiting, of wondering about the new life in Dove Woman's belly.

"Oh, look," she exclaimed suddenly, pointing to an area near the stream.

A cow elk had come down to the water to drink. She raised her head and sniffed the breeze, catching the scent of the couple who watched. They were near enough to see the droplets of water that dribbled down the animal's lower lip. The cow fidgeted, uneasy but undecided.

It was unusual for elk to approach the village this closely. The cow was in no danger at this time, but she could hardly know that. The People had hunted well, with the greening of the prairie. White Buffalo had selected the time for the annual burning of the prairie to remove the winter's dead grass. The buffalo had appeared as expected, in the Moon of Greening. The spring hunt had been successful enough to add prestige to White Buffalo's reputation and respect for the power of his medicine. Successful enough that there would be no interest in killing a thin cow elk during the calving season.

The cow turned nervously, sensing something wrong, and finally sprang away, clattering across the white gravel of the riffle toward the other bank. Only then, as she turned and made a quiet, lowing sound over her shoulder, did they see the calf. It came scrambling up out of the tall grass beside the stream, a confused scramble of long legs, knobby knees and floppy ears.

The mother paused to wait a moment, while the calf

stumbled after her through the shallows. They quickly disappeared in the willows across the creek, and Dove Woman laughed softly.

"It is a sign, my husband."

"Your time is near?"

"Maybe so."

She smiled and leaned against him.

So, looking into the face of his son the following day, White Buffalo realized that the incident by the stream *had* been significant. Dove Woman had felt it, too, and had chosen this name. He nodded in agreement.

" 'Small Elk'. It is good."

As the child grew, White Buffalo wondered sometimes if he had been mistaken. Small Elk seemed much like other children, no better or worse, no more or less mischievous. He participated in the games, dances, and instruction of the Rabbit Society with the other children. But no, there was, in addition, that other quality, the desire of this child to sometimes be alone, to watch ants or silvery minnows in the stream, or the red-tailed hawk's lazy circles in the summer sky.

When Small Elk was in his fourth summer, he came to his father one afternoon with a small object in his closed hand. His face was shining with excitement. White Buffalo was reclining on his willow back-rest, enjoying a smoke during a moment of leisure.

"What do you have there, littie one?"

"It is a stone," the child confided in hushed excitement. "Its spirit is good."

White Buffalo became more attentive. This was not the usual play of a three-year-old.

"May I hold it?"

Small Elk proudly placed the stone in his father's palm. It was white and rounded, polished by many lifetimes of tumbling in the rolling waters of the stream. White Buffalo closed his fingers around the smooth sphere, thinking as he did that it was much like an egg. The egg, perhaps, of one of the small ducks that sometimes nested in the reeds along the stream. It was warm, and the feeling was good.

"Yes," he told the child, "its spirit is good."

"Father, do all things have a spirit?"

"Yes. Some are stronger spirits than others."

"But this is a good spirit?"

White Buffalo felt the smooth surface in his palm, the warm, comforting sensation that was unmistakable.

"Yes," he said seriously, "this is good."

"I will keep it," Small Elk announced happily.

White Buffalo was still a little surprised that he was carrying on this conversation with a child of three. However, his expertise with things of the spirit told him not to ignore it. Small Elk was showing signs of spiritual awakening quite early. It might be that this child would be offered the power of a strong medicine when he was ready. If, of course, he chose to accept the responsibility of such a gift. The idea pleased the holy man, that a son of his might follow in his steps. But for now . . .

"Come," he said to Small Elk, "let us make for you a medicine bag. Your stone will be its first spirit."

It would not do to try to influence the boy. However, it would do no harm to make the means available to him, if and when he was offered the gift. After all, he could still refuse the responsibility, if he wished.

2

» » »

Small Elk sat on the grassy slope with the other children of the Rabbit Society. One of the women was demonstrating the use of the throwing stick. She was holding a stick not quite as long as her arm and of the thickness of her wrist. A few steps away, slender willow twigs had been stuck in the mud to form a miniature fence as a target.

"Now, see!"

Bluebird suddenly whirled her arm and released the stick in a hard overhand throw. The missile whirled, end over end, at the willow target, knocking one of the slim twigs flat as it bounced beyond. The children laughed happily. One of the boys ran to retrieve her stick.

"Now, see again!" She called as she readied the stick for another throw.

This time the throw was a side-arm swing. The club-like stick spun horizontally, whirring toward the row of twigs. When it struck, the damage was apparent. Because of the flat spin, not one, but several of the willow twigs were broken or knocked flat, in a path two hand-spans wide.

"So," Bluebird announced, "you will kill more rabbits with the side-throw. Now, try it. Don't hit each other!"

"When can we try the bow?" asked Red Fox.

"Later. Soon, maybe, if you have one. But, it is good to know the throwing sticks."

"But I would rather eat buffalo than rabbit," one of the girls protested.

"So would everyone," Bluebird agreed. "But, when meat is scarce, in the Moon of Hunger, it is good to know how to hunt with the stick. Or, when the hunters are unsuccessful. Then what?"

The children took their small throwing sticks and began to play at hunting rabbits. Bluebird walked over to speak to her friend Dove Woman, who sat watching.

"I will stand clear now," she laughed. "They are reckless sometimes."

Dove Woman smiled.

"At least, the dance is not so dangerous."

Hers was the teaching of the first dance steps to the smaller children of the Rabbit Society. From others they would learn the skills of hunting and the use of weapons, and compete in running, wrestling, and swimming. Both boys and girls learned all of these skills. It was not until later that their diversity of interests would sharpen the fine skills of the hunter-warriors, and the domestic skills of the young women planning for their own lodges.

There was a yelp from one of the dogs, hit by an accidental bounce of a thrown stick.

"Be careful, there!" called Bluebird.

Then she spoke an aside to Dove Woman.

"Better a dog than each other. Now they will be more careful."

"Yes. There is no way to keep dogs away from throwing sticks, I think."

"Your Small Elk seems good with the sticks."

"Thank you. Your daughter, also."

Dove Woman was pleased. These two children, Small Elk and Crow, were nearly the same age. Their mothers were friends, and usually chose to set up their lodges near each other.

"They play well together," Bluebird observed.

"Yes, for children of five summers, they quarrel very little."

Both women laughed.

"Will your Small Elk become a medicine man?" Bluebird asked seriously.

"Who knows?" Dove Woman shrugged. "White Buffalo says he may. We will see if he has the gift."

The children were becoming tired of playing with the sticks now, and were straying off to other pursuits. Small Elk and Crow were near the stream, sitting on a level rock. Between them were a number of miniature green lodges, made by rolling cottonwood leaves into cones and pinning the edges together with a grass stem.

"Let us make a whole village!" Crow suggested.

"Why? We need only one lodge, you and I."

Then they both giggled.

"Elk, do you know how to make a moccasin from a cottonwood leaf?"

"No. I have seen them. It is harder than making the little lodges."

"You could ask your father. He knows all things."

"Yes, but. . . . "

Small Elk was a little uncertain whether a holy man's area of skills included the making of toy cottonwood-leaf moccasins.

"I will ask, some time," he agreed cautiously.

The conversation was interrupted by the approach of one of the other boys.

"Want to go swimming?" asked Bull Roarer.

He stood there, whirling a noise-maker on a thong, around and around his head in a wide circle. With each revolution, the flutter of the flattened stick at the thong's end made a deep whirring noise, like the distant bellow of a buffalo bull. It was a common toy, but this boy's affinity for the pastime had led to his being called by the name of the device, "bull roarer".

"Who is going?" Crow asked.

Bull Roarer continued to swing his noise maker.

"We three, Fox, Otter, Cat-tail, my sister Redwing."

"We will ask," Crow announced.

She jumped up and ran to her mother with the explanation and request. Bull Roarer's sister was a few summers older, a reliable supervisor, and both Bluebird and Dove Woman quickly agreed.

Most children of the People were strong swimmers. The

bands must always camp near a water supply, and summer camp was frequently selected with an eye to its recreational possibilities. Of course, this went hand in hand with the more serious purpose of the selection, availability of game. Grass and water, essential to the buffalo, also make a camp site esthetically pleasing. In turn, the presence of a clear, cool stream in the heat of a prairie summer invites swimmers.

The summer camp this season was in a favorite area of the People. Sycamore River, trickling over white gravel bars and long level shelves of gray slate, was a favorite stream. Its deep pools were spaced at intervals along its course like beads on a thong. The pool the children preferred was perhaps two long bow shots below the camp. It was ringed with willows on the near side, except for a level strip of white gravelly sand, a perfect place to lie in the sun to dry after a swim. Across the pool, a stone's throw away, cat tails formed a backdrop for the scene, as well as a site where ducks and smaller water-dwelling birds might build their lodges.

The memorable event of the day for Small Elk, however, was not the swimming party. It happened on the way back to the camp. He and Crow had lagged behind the others to watch a shiny green dung beetle roll an impossibly big ball of dung, larger than itself.

"What do they do with it?" asked Crow. "Where is he taking it?"

"To his lodge, maybe," Small Elk suggested.

He hated to admit that he had no idea what a dung beetle does with balls of dung. He would ask his father later. White Buffalo, who knew all things, could surely tell him about dung beetles.

The children rose to move on. It was just at that time that the rabbit sprang from a clump of grass beside the path and loped away ahead of them. Small Elk was startled for a moment, but then reacted almost without thinking. He was still carrying his throwing-stick from the earlier lessons of the day. The missile leaped from his hand, whirling toward the retreating animal. His throw was wide, and should have missed completely except for unforeseen circumstances. The whirling tip of the stick struck a sapling beside the path and was deflected, bouncing crazily end over end. Even so, the rabbit would have escaped harm if it had continued in a straight line. But rabbits do not run in straight lines as a usual custom. They sometimes zig and zag, taught to do so at the time of creation to escape the strike of the hawk or the lunge of the coyote. In this case, the escape trick proved the rabbit's undoing. It bobbed to the left just as the whirling stick bounced to the right. There was an audible crack as the hard wood met the skull of the animal.

"Aiee!" exclaimed Crow softly.

Small Elk rushed forward to grab the kicking creature, wriggling in its death-throes. He picked it up and watched the large brown eye lose its lustre and become dull with the mist of death. It was his first kill, and he should have felt good. It should be a glad and proud moment, but that was not what he felt. There was a let-down, a disappointment. The rabbit had been more pleasing to look at in life than it was now, with the eyes glazing and a single drop of blood at the tip of its nose. He was confused. Why had he wanted to kill the rabbit? For meat. Yes, for its flesh, he thought. That is the way of things. The rabbit eats grass, and in turn is eaten by the hawk, the coyote, or by man. That is the purpose of a rabbit. He watched as a flea crept into sight from the thick fur of the rabbit's cheek and burrowed into another tuft.

Then he remembered watching his father at a buffalo kill early in the spring. The medicine man had stood before the head of a massive bull. . . . yes, of course. He would perform such a ceremony. He placed the rabbit on the ground, arranging it in a natural position. Then he stepped back, faced the head of the dead creature, and addressed it solemnly.

"I am sorry to kill you, my brother," he stated, trying to remember his father's words of apology, "but I am in need of your flesh to live."

He felt a little guilty for such a statement, because he was not hungry or in need at the moment. What had White Buffalo said next?

"Your flesh feeds us as the grass gives your life to you."

Yes, that was it. Small Elk felt better now, and forged ahead. How was it?

"May your people be fat and happy, and be plentiful," he told the rabbit.

Feeling considerably better about the incident, he picked up his kill and moved on toward camp. In his preoccupation, he did not notice the expression in the eyes of the girl beside him. It was an intense look of surprise mixed with admiration and approval.

A similar expression might have been noted on the face of the man who had watched the whole scene from behind a thin screen of willow. White Buffalo waited, perfectly still until the children had moved on out of sight. Then he rose, a satisfied smile on his face. He must share this with Dove Woman.

"It is good," he said quietly to himself. "And, Small Elk performed the apology well."

About the Author

»»»

DON COLDSMITH was born in Iola, Kansas, in 1926. He served as a World War II combat medic in the South Pacific and returned to his native state where he graduated from Baker University in 1949 and received his M.D. from the University of Kansas in 1958. He worked at several jobs before entering medical school: he was a YMCA group counselor, a gunsmith, a taxidermist, and for a short time, a Congregational preacher. In addition to his private medical practice, Dr. Coldsmith is a staff physician at Emporia State University's Health Center, teaches in the English Department, and is active as a freelance writer, lecturer, and rancher. He and his wife of 26 years, Edna, have raised five daughters.

Dr. Coldsmith produced the first ten novels in "The Spanish Bit Saga" in a five-year period; he writes and revises the stories first in his head, then in longhand. From this manuscript he reads aloud to his wife, whom he calls his "chief editor." Finally the finished version is skillfully typed by his longtime office receptionist.

Of his decision to create, or re-create, the world of the Plains Indian in the 16th and 17th centuries, the author says: "There has been very little written about this time period. I wanted also to portray these native Americans as human beings, rather than as stereotyped 'Indians.' That word does not appear anywhere in the series—for a reason. As I have researched the time and place, the indigenous cultures, it's been a truly inspiring experience for me."

A Proud People In a Harsh Land

THE SPANISH BIT SAGA

Set on the Great Plains of America in the early 16th century, Don Coldsmith's acclaimed series recreates a time, a place and a people that have been nearly lost to history. With the advent of the Spaniards, the horse culture came to the people of the Plains. Here is history in the making through the eyes of the proud Native Americans who lived it.

- ☐ BOOK 1: TRAIL OF THE SPANISH BIT 26397 $2.95
- ☐ BOOK 2: THE ELK-DOG HERITAGE 26412 $2.95
- ☐ BOOK 3: FOLLOW THE WIND 26806 $2.95
- ☐ BOOK 4: BUFFALO MEDICINE 26938 $2.95
- ☐ BOOK 5: MAN OF THE SHADOWS 27607 $2.95
- ☐ BOOK 6: DAUGHTER OF THE EAGLE 27209 $2.95
- ☐ BOOK 7: MOON OF THE THUNDER 27344 $2.95
- ☐ BOOK 8: SACRED HILLS 27460 $2.95
- ☐ BOOK 9: PALE STAR 27604 $2.95
- ☐ BOOK 10: RIVER OF SWANS 27708 $2.95
- ☐ BOOK 11: RETURN TO THE RIVER 28163 $2.95

**FROM THE PRODUCER OF WAGONS WEST
AND THE KENT FAMILY CHRONICLES—
A SWEEPING SAGA OF WAR AND HEROISM
AT THE BIRTH OF A NATION**

THE WHITE INDIAN SERIES

This thrilling series tells the compelling story of America's birth against the equally exciting adventures of an English child raised as a Seneca.

☐	24650	White Indian #1	$3.95
☐	25020	The Renegade #2	$3.95
☐	24751	War Chief #3	$3.95
☐	24476	The Sachem #4	$3.95
☐	25154	Renno #5	$3.95
☐	25039	Tomahawk #6	$3.95
☐	25589	War Cry #7	$3.95
☐	25202	Ambush #8	$3.95
☐	23986	Seneca #9	$3.95
☐	24492	Cherokee #10	$3.95
☐	24950	Choctaw #11	$3.95
☐	25353	Seminole #12	$3.95
☐	25868	War Drums #13	$3.95
☐	26206	Apache #14	$3.95
☐	27161	Spirit Knife #15	$3.95
☐	27264	Manitou #16	$3.95
☐	27814	Seneca Warrior #17	$3.95

Bantam Books, Dept. LE3, 414 East Golf Road, Des Plaines, IL 60016

Please send me the items I have checked above. I am enclosing $_____ (please add $2.00 to cover postage and handling). Send check or money order, no cash or C.O.D.s please.

Mr/Ms _____

Address _____

City/State _____ Zip_____

LE3-9/89

Please allow four to six weeks for delivery.
Prices and availability subject to change without notice.